Ho… Get *Here?*

A Novella

Ahmad Williams

MORTIFIED BOOKS
2101 Commons Road South
Reynoldsburg, OHIO 43068

HOW DID I GET *HERE?*

This book is a work of fiction. Names, characters, and incidents are simply products of the author's imagination. Any resemblance to actual events, places, the living or dead, is entirely coincidental.

For more information, please contact Mortified Books at:
mortifiedbooks@gmail.com

Book Cover, Publisher Logo, and Interior Layout & Design:
Scribe Freelance | www.scribefreelance.com

ISBN: 978-0-9825564-0-5

Printed in the United States of America

To my sister Keeva Lynn Williams . . . who I never grew very close to here on earth, but who continues to feel closer to me everyday that goes by as I recall her quiet spirit that will endure forever.

Acknowledgements

First and foremost I have to thank and give all praises to God who has blessed me with so many gifts that I continue to discover. This is my first book and there are so many inspirations out there that I could go on about forever.

Thinking back to the beginning of this trek I have to thank my beautiful wife Crystal for instilling in me the belief that I could write a book worth reading. After hesitating for a year, I have finally taken her advice and have been more than blessed by the outcome of this work.

I would love to thank all of my family in New Jersey for helping mold me into the man that I have become today. To all of my children will continually fill my heart and who I think and pray about 24/7. Without any of you, I am not sure if I would have a life worth living for. Your smiles and your high expectations of Daddy will always inspire me to do better than I originally think.

To Cliff, Donnie, John John, Shaka, Andrea, Sonya, Audrey, Linda, Jessica, Valerie, and Wanda. You all knew me ever since I played Midget Football in Vineland. I could never for get your support, love, and persistent encouragement for me to always to better.

Dad, the wisdom you continuously pumped into my brain could never have a price tag on it. You never missed an opportunity to have the video camera on us whenever you could so that we could enjoy so many of those films today. You are not only a father to us, but you continue to be a father to all of those who never had the privilege that we all witnessed. I can't believe how time has flown by and how we grew up so fast, but those quotes never grow old; because I can still hear them as if I were sitting at that kitchen table in Brotmanville, New Jersey on a Sunday morning. If anyone ever asks me I continue to tell them that you were my first barber, pastor, professor, architect, electrician, and favorite orator. You were the one that has always inspired me to go out and do things myself rather than depend on someone else.

Mom, who could ever forget all of the sacrifices that you continue to display on a daily basis? The persistent love that you have shown me, even in my time enlisted in the devil's army you continued to hug me and tell me there are better days to come. Anytime I look at you, I can only think that heaven must be a wonderful place to be, because to smile after such sacrifice does not come easy.

To all of my friends at Ohio State, Syracuse, and Arthur P. Schalick High School, I love you and continue to reflect on those experiences we have shared as I put my gift of writing to work through the love of you all.

If there is anyone that I have forgotten, I am sure that this will not be my final book and that I am truly sorry and please do not hold it against me; my gratitude could never be extended enough.

Author's Note

We currently live in a time where brokenness has gone unnoticed and where immoralities are so influenced by Hollywood; that the rest of the world does not recognize it is that very stigma that continues to crush our God-given purposes in life. The sin of it all, is that we think that there's nothing wrong!

I can not express enough how every decision that we make as human beings are so critical to those that come after us. It may not seem like much at the time, but some of our decisions affect children generations long after we are gone from this place. It is said that the average human being affects 10,000 people! Could you imagine that? Just think of yourself in an open field and picture 10,000 people behind you. It's an overwhelming thought, but we are all critical beings in this day and age called, life.

As we embark on the journey of this three part series, we will explore the ride of Preston Brown. Preston is not different from many men in today's world. He struggles with the same issues, endures the same temptations, and has the same interests that many men do; regardless of race, economic status, or location. We will see how he twists and turns through all of the situations that he may encounter. Although, Preston is impressive, he makes some very unpopular mistakes that may make you cringe, cry, and even make you laugh. Reading Preston's story will reveal to you that even the most polished of human beings can make mistakes, but the story does not have to end there!

In the Beginning

In the Beginning

I tell you what: this *brother Preston has the perfect life. He is intelligent, smart, athletic, compassionate, and did I mention intelligent? He has everything a twenty five year old man would want in his life a wife, house, kids, and a dog. Now how many brothers in America can sting with that? Not to mention that he is on the verge of finishing his master's degree; in seminary! I have never seen someone so driven and persistent to defy all of the odds against him every waking day of his life. I can remember our last year at Ohio State together; Preston completed 67 hours in one school year! For those of you who don't know 67 hours is the equivalent of two school years, in fact there are some that go to school for 4 years and don't get that much done. He is more than dangerous, he is straight driven!*

Oh, yeah excuse my manners but I'm Preston's conscience and we have been hanging strong now for just about twenty five years and counting. But, I don't think Preston noticed me until he was about three years old. I have always been there for him, but like most men he doesn't always listen to me and somehow I end up paying all of the consequences along with him. Now getting back to the dangerous Mr. Preston; the man works out like an unbelievable animal. Preston is six feet tall, 220 pounds (85% muscle), caramel colored, sports a low fade, and a million dollar smile that is contagious to everyone he encounters. He's always casually dressed, never saggin in his pants (he thinks it's tacky) and not ashamed to wear some ten dollar shoes purchased at Wal-Mart and wear them like he bought them from Sean John himself!

Preston is an officer in the Army and is on his way to into the Army Chaplaincy. It is just amazing how he can stay in school, married with two kids, and still finds a way to get things done. God must really have something on hold of him, because every time there is more work to do he just prays longer and we both get through it as if there was nothing to it. His ambition is to one day become a politician to fight many of the atrocities that are imposed on families that reside in the inner city. The passion that he has for human life is great and runs deep within his daily walk! But in the meantime, it is no problem to just sit back and budget the food stamps with his lovely wife and scrape the bottom of the barrel to see how once again the rent is going to be paid. I must admit, Preston does love raising his children in Columbus, Ohio. It is a lot better than where he and his wife use to live back in Vineland, New Jersey. The cost of living was outrageous and the car insurance was unbelievable. Nevertheless, Preston could never forget all of the friends he made in Vineland

and Brotmanville growing up. After all, his South Jersey slang and keen sense of humor is what attracts people toward him. In addition, who would go anywhere else other than Ohio State? The football games, the possible connections, and all of the festivities that go on in the city just couldn't be passed up. We barely made it out of Jersey on our own terms, because someone decided to frame us with a beating in Millville the night before we caught the Greyhound to Ohio. After two days on campus, don't you know that the State Trooper was calling the dorm room asking about coming in for a polygraph test! This even shook me for a minute, because getting involved with law enforcement is just something we do not do. I mean, Preston didn't even have any traffic tickets in his name. But, that's Jersey for you, when you're trying to make it, there is always someone else watching and waiting to tear you down. After the third day on campus, when it was confirmed that he was at a girlfriend's house and Mama Brown cussing out the trooper over the phone, Preston and I never heard any more of it. To this day, we still don't know who told that story and the bizarre thing about it is that the law had his mama's license plate number of the minivan he was driving that night!

Now that all of that is behind us, things were supposed to get easier, but somehow men just love to make the easy things that much more compli-

cated on themselves. Well, I am Preston's conscience and I will promise to tell him the truth, nothing but the truth, so help me God! Like I said I will always say what is on my mind, but if Preston chooses to refute me or not is totally up to him and the good Lord Himself! The man does seem to have the perfect life doesn't he, but I promise you the test of time has yet to come as we will see how my man is faced with the mother of all scandals in his life and how he chooses to deal with it. Soon he will know what decisions are really his and which ones are definitely God's. Enjoy!

Chapter I

Preston has a beautiful wife named Delight, and delightful to the eye she is. A short, slender woman standing about five feet two inches tall, long jet black hair like a stallion and the perfect set of calves that were not too big or too small, but looked like little ant hills on her legs. She was a perfect mix of African-American and Puerto Rican descent and whoever her parents were blended so nicely together. She loves to play with their children, and she especially loved to kiss on her husband in public. She had no problem letting everyone know the she was, is, and always will be Mrs. Brown. Delight Brown is older than Preston, but only looks about eighteen years old and with a size four waist that made men always take a double take when out in public. Preston never was the jealous type, he was too spoiled in high school being the man in every sport including the band, not to mention some football early on in college, but injury changed that whole story quickly. Mrs. Brown will always be the one that has his back no matter what the circumstances and being the typical Jersey girl, confrontation is not an issue. The confrontation thing could get a little out of hand, because in general men don't like to be challenged in front of their children once something is put into place by the "king of the castle". But, some women get it and some don't, but in all sorts that's why they call it marriage. Because once you decide to get married, you have officially declared war on yourself! I don't mean that figuratively either, I am talking physically, emotionally, spiritually, and every other brink of the surface imaginable. Preston feels that once the law is laid down there should be no compromise in the word spoken, but it tends to differ once you marry a strong, African-American woman. Not to mention a strong Latino background. So fellas out there, you know there is plenty of opportunity for the house to get real loud real quick with a neighbor in the apartment complex next door ready to call the cops or put a glass up to the wall.

The greatest of confrontations happened while Preston watched the kids on Monday night; while Delight went to school. Going to school on Monday nights at Ohio Dominican University afforded Delight the opportunity to go back to school since she worked throughout high school to take care of her oldest son Simon. The kids were acting up more than typical kids that night and Preston finally had enough. He sent the kids to bed without any milk and cookies.

"That's it, that's it that is it!" Preston blasted. "Take y'all behinds to bed and don't think you gonna come downstairs when mom get home thinking everything all peaches and cream." The boys knew once it was "daddy night" there was no turning against the word and if there were it would be nothing but a butt whooping to end the conversation. So the boys with a defeated look on their faces, put their heads down in utter disgust and walked up the steps as slowly as possible to go upstairs. Typically, when things are going good it only takes about three seconds for the boys to run upstairs inside the two-bedroom townhome in Canal Winchester. But, since dad wasn't playing around it was time to get crackin up the stairs quickly! Anyone could admit that Preston and his wife had a pretty nice apartment. The boys both shared a room, but they were only eight and five so it wasn't like they were on the verge of puberty wanting their own space. They loved making each other miserable and hated separation. Upstairs was very beautiful inside; the master bedroom the room was so wide open it was hard to believe that it wasn't the living room upstairs! A fresh carpet, a walk-in closet, and a nice double sink with the toilet and bathtub; both in another room all by itself. Preston loved that part of the house, that way he could hide away whenever he needed to.

And oh my goodness, the central air was lovely, it was self regulated and the bill was never too high. All of the walls were a neutral color and Delight could decorate it whenever and however she wanted to. She wasn't much of a wall decorator to begin with, but she just loved to have the option anyway. The greatest part that the Browns loved was that they had their very own bathroom and the boys had theirs. This was especially great for a very kinky night when the children were all sound to sleep and no waking surprises in sight. To cap off a romantic night was the way that the sun rose every morning in their room. Looking out of the window, you could see across a big field and it would look like the apartment was telling the sun to rise and they were the only beings on Earth God every created.

10 o'clock finally rolled around and any minute Delight would be walking through the garage door to greet Preston. Finally, Preston heard the garage close and sees Delight as sexy as their wedding night and without looking for two seconds . . .

"Mommy, we missed you!" blurts out Simon, the older of the two. Simon was very clever whenever it was time to go to bed, because he could make it seem like that he was starved by old dad or that he stayed up almost home sick to see mom come back home; even though he knew that bedtime was at 8 o'clock. You see, Simon was Preston's step son ever since he was two, so being the new man coming in always made it some sort of dilemma going on with the power struggle in the house. The over protective mom and the singled out stepson; it was a classic American family.

"I thought I told y'all to go to bed an hour ago? No one told y'all to come downstairs when mom came home!! See ya, peace, be gone!" Preston blared nonchalantly.

Simon glanced at Delight with puppy eyes before he turned his back towards the kitchen like an orphan on one of those missionary commercials that you see 4 o'clock Sunday morning on TBN.

"Papi, you don't have to go anywhere give mommy hug. Did you guys get milk and cookies?"

"Hell no they didn't get any milk and cookies and Tiger shouldn't be downstairs!" Preston blurted out.

Delight frowned and said, "Well it's a tradition that we all have in my family and I always give them milk and cookies before they go to bed."

"I already told them no and I don't think that it is appropriate to override what I say in front of the kids, I told you about that numerous times before and you just can't seem to get that through your little head, you know what, bump it, let them do whatever they want the rest of the night."

"Don't get an attitude, because you know that's what I do with them."

"Oh no, I don't have an attitude about the cookies, I have an attitude about the crap that you just pulled out of your butt less than a minute ago", Preston huffed. Preston's eyes were real narrow and it's a stitch of anger that rarely comes out of Preston when he is more than a little upset. . . . And wham! The chair goes tumbling across the kitchen and living room floor, knocking over the lamp stand, coffee table in the living room, and almost taking out the patio door. Whenever Preston gets mad, Delight has no problem rising to the occasion in trying to show her equal position in the house.

"Well if that's what you wanna do well stay yourself downstairs on the couch and I will take myself to sleep comfortably", Delight proudly announced. Preston sometimes just wanted to grab her by the face and just choke slam her, but he knew he could already beat her in a fight and that he would feel like an idiot once he did it, so once again he just let the thought go.

"Alright, go upstairs and don't ask me to get anything out of the kitchen in the middle of the night, because I really don't want to answer anyone that can't listen to their husband, when I can get a whole bunch of strange women to listen to me in a classroom!" *Preston you know you shouldn't have said that. That could mean a shoe, a pan, or something that will just prolong the night.* Preston knew he was wrong, but he really knew this could strike a nerve to get Delight's attention at some point and time, so he just stayed on the couch with a grin on his face waiting for that famous thumping of the feet down the stairs and waiting for those famous words. . . .

"What did you say? I think you better take that back?" Delight snickered to Preston with her finger on his nose. She knew that Preston hated fingers in front of his face and Delight wanted him just to do something that would give her a reason to go off. She straddled him on the couch with her celadon Victoria's secret lingerie outfit that she just bought for his birthday last week. She was small enough to fit just about anywhere and she cornered him on the couch and only the dog could watch and the kids listened upstairs. She pushed her finger up to forehead like she was his drill sergeant and said, "Mr. Brown, listen up and listen real good, the next time you want to go comparing your wife to some ditzy school girls, you're going to wish your mom was here to save you. She will have a dead son and I will have no remorse; you hear me?"

"Yeah, okay. And the boys will have no parents, because mom will straight kill you three times the same way she wanted to kill you when you finally told us about Squire. Yeah, you forgot all about that didn't you? Just because we married doesn't mean you did anything any better, girl you been trippin', just act like you wanna get dumb and see how it goes down in this joint tonight!" Preston threw Delight off of him like a little rag doll and rolled over on the couch to go to sleep.

Delight hopped on his back and commenced to repeatedly smack him in the back of the head, while Preston laughed in between his elbows and shook his head in bewilderment. After Delight ran out of breath she huffed and stomped up the stairs and slammed the door. *Now that was not the thing to do, especially when a romantic night is brewing, we've been celibate for three days and that was not the way to cap it off. Go upstairs in about two hours and throw that lingerie off to the side and make magic tonight! Preston just listen to me this one time, let your pride down and do something that will look past all of that anger, come on; do it for us.*

After about five hours Preston decided to go upstairs and romanticize his wife. He crept up the stairs very slowly, taking off each article of clothing with each step he took upstairs. He creeked the door open slowly to see his beautiful gift from God sleeping as if she were waiting for him to come from behind and caress her. She really was one of the most beautiful creatures that God has ever created, but she just gets on my last nerve sometimes, Preston thought. Well, at this point it was show time and Preston had to fulfill his duty as husband and off to an intimate night he went.

Chapter II

The sun shone brightly through the window the following morning and it was just about time to get Simon and Squire some cereal before they had to run off to school. Preston hated waking them up in the morning, but since he didn't have to be anywhere until about 10a.m. he figured it just helped him sneak in some more quality time with Delight.

"Rise and shine soldiers!" Preston yelled. He knew that really got on the kids nerves every Tuesday morning so he kind of got a kick out of it. "Those boys sure do know how to stay up late at night and have the nerve to try and act like they are tired in the morning" he yelled to Delight from the hallway.

"They better get out of here, because I am not getting out of this bed as sore as I am to try and run them to school this morning", Delight added hastily. "I am as tired and sore as three football players after an NFL playoff game. My thighs feel like they took a pounding. When you go in overdrive you have no regard for human life!"

Preston liked it when Delight boosted his ego every now and then. It made him feel like he was worth something and that there was some sense of control that he owned in the household. *It made us feel like King of the Jungle!!!!!!!!* That's all a black man ever wanted every now and again was a little respect. Not let me walk all over you, but respect my ground and acknowledge me when I put in a little work, Preston pondered. He was so lost in her words that it sent him into a deep daydreaming spell of what the perfect marriage was supposed to be like.

"Uh-Umm", Delight snarled snapping Preston out of his daydream. "We have to discuss some of your attitude from last night."

"Oh boy, here we go . . ." Preston replied rubbing his head and wondering what she was going to come up with now. Every time they got done having sex it always seemed like Delight found it to be the most opportune time to interrupt his flow of a perfect beginning. "Okay let me have it" Preston stated in a defeated tone.

"See you're starting already. Every time we get ready to have a serious conversation you just want to say whatever I want to hear just to get the conversation over with" Delight yelled with her forehead at his chin. "Every time you get some you start acting stupid like you just had the "get dumb" with Delight juice. Just because we have sex doesn't mean it solves all of our problems. Well, if you don't want to talk

about it just go ahead and do what you going to do this morning and don't think you going to be getting some any time soon".
Before she could finish Preston already had his book bag on and was on his way out the door with his keys dangling to put in the ignition. She is so good to kiss on, but a ridiculous nag when it comes to the minutest things that don't go her way, Preston thought. "I'm sure that the cell phone will soon be ringing at least eight times before I even get down the street."
Preston why don't you just listen to her and hear her out sometime before you go storming out the door like that? You know that she won't let it go until you open yourself up and address the issue.
But when I address the issue she finds a way to make it like she is the one that is always right and she tries to argue me down about how wrong I am and the conversation just goes her way anyway if we are at it long enough, Preston kept replaying in his mind.

The cell phone began to vibrate in Preston's pocket once again and he couldn't believe it . . . three voice mails already since he got down the road! Preston figured she would just cool down after a little while and just leave the cell phone at Delight's mercy. Preston just couldn't figure out what it was about women and cell phones. Sometimes they would call and text so much that it would make someone just want to throw it out the window and feel the freedom from the thing for a few hours. But, no excuse exists for saying I threw the cell phone away for awhile and Preston is sure that no female could ever believe that. It's a nice day here today in Columbus, Preston twirled in his mind as he blasted Da Truth in his CD player on the way to school. "As a matter of fact it is so nice, that I think I will give Longs a call and see if he wants to play a little bit of Playstation 3".

Longs has been one of Preston's best friends ever since they started seminary together. Knowing Longs was more than a blessing. For one, Longs was born and raised in Columbus and he graduated from Wilberforce University with a computer science degree. Everyone knows that in this day and age of computer programming there is lots of money to be saved when you know someone personally that can handle all of your IT problems. If there was ever a problem Preston had personally, financially, or humanly; Longs was there to help out any way that he could in any capacity. To make short work of it, Longs was down for whatever Preston had going on.

Longs had his own house, the only child, and only one son to take care of. Some would say that he is spoiled, but Preston would just say that his mom and dad were real good at making plans together. He was ten years Preston's senior, but spiritually they could speak about anything and could say anything to each other; because they worked on a straight "keeping it real" basis. In other words, confidentiality and vulnerability was not at all foreign to in their relationship to one another. Although, it was cool with Preston, Delight really didn't like the fact that he was single, had his own house, and multiple women in and out of his life like music CD's. But she could appreciate the fact that Preston knew someone that wouldn't charge an arm and a leg to get the computer fixed if need be.

"What's going' on black man?" Longs yawned into the phone.

"Nothin', bout to swing your way to see if you wanna get whooped up on some Madden since I'm not going to my first class."

"Come on I'll be right here on Deshler in the basement cat!"

"Aight. I'm headed down the Pike right now getting ready to jump on 104. Peace."

For Longs getting a game on the big screen in the basement was never a problem. He loved the fact that he could sit down with someone black and could talk politics about the poverty that went on in the country affecting the black community on a consistent basis. Not to mention their theological debates on the latest subject in class. Is the New Testament absolute truth? Why do we Christians even bother with the Old Testament? If it's so old, why do we take bits and pieces out of the Bible and not just make it all anew? Those were just a couple of the questions that turned into seminary career debates between the two of them.

BAM! BAM! BAM!

"Hold on black man", Longs yelled up the stairs to come open up the door on the side of the house. "Man, I told you to just open the door, I unlocked it when I got off the phone with you!"

"Oh, my bad I didn't hear you say anything over the phone, I guess I just had a weak signal on the way in."

"No, before I could call you back, you left your Blackberry on and I heard you singing every damn song on the Tom Joyner Morning Show", Longs replied irritably. "Anyway, what brings you on down with such short notice? I know something on your mind, because any other time I can't beg you to take a break from that seminary library. I didn't think all of that reading in the world could help me remember a thing", Longs nodded with his head in between his legs with the joystick.

"Well, once again your prediction is on point and I am just getting so sick of Delight giving me a headache every time we get done doing the nasty. I mean, I watch the kids while she's in school, the house is clean, and she still finds something to rant and rave about. So I just had to get out of the house and relieve some stress for a couple of hours and there was no way that I could just sit in there another minute while she yelled up and down my neck like I stole her hair conditioner or something."

"But you have to think about it like this Preston. She just got home from class and that's the only place where she can actually socialize outside of church and she was probably stressed out after dealing with that crazy cohort group of hers she keeps complaining to me about when I go over there. See, you don't get. You don't know how to let a woman talk and keep your damn mouth shut until she done and you just finish the conversation with a simple, "okay". But no! You gotta be Super Negro exchanging lyrical blows with the wife left and right until you find yourself over here playing some video games like your sons will be doing in a few hours," Longs said with a smile. Longs knew that he was getting into Preston's head, because Longs just scored on an interception and ran a kickoff back upon recovery. What made it worse was that Preston was playing with the Eagles against Longs' faithful Cleveland Browns.

"I don't know how I'm lettin' you beat up on me with a sorry Ohio NFL team. The only thing professional in this state are the Buckeyes and they can barely show up when it's time to get into a championship game" Preston slammed down the joystick in cheerful disgust.

"It sounds like your cell phone going off you might want to answer it", Longs said eyeing the flashing red light from the Blackberry that kept disturbing him in the dimly lit basement.

"Man, I have been avoiding that for the last hour, let me turn this thing off so I can keep my sanity. I meant to keep it in the car until I got ready to go to the afternoon class. This is the last week before finals so I don't even know if I'm goin' to hit that one up." *Preston you know you are the only black person in that class and everyone will know that you are the only one missing if you don't go.* "As a matter of fact, I think I will go, because the devil ain't about to take me down, he just gonna get another egg in his face after this round", Preston stood up confidently getting his bag ready to head out the door.

"Awe, here you go trying to run out of the door just because you getting whooped up on like Big Daddy on his baby last night," Longs said waving his hand back and forth across his mid section. "Anyway, I might be up there a little later on so if you go the computer lab save me a seat, because you know most of the white folks at the seminary don't care for me, because I tell it how it is."

"Aight, but if you don't show up you know you sold me out like a Tyler Perry movie on Friday night", Preston smirked on his way to the car in the driveway. "Tell your mom, dad, and little man I said what's up."

CHAPTER III

This Christian Ethics class is boring, Preston thought to himself seated in the front row of the classroom. What does it really matter if a female is trying to stay from an unwanted pregnancy by taking some birth control pills? Is it more Christian to get pregnant during high school and have a baby?

"And that is what the Christian pastor in today's world is called to address in the context of the 21st century," the red headed female instructor concluded. "Well, this quarter has been lots of fun and remember to email me all of your finals exams that must be at least 6-8 pages addressing one of the discussion questions I have listed on the sheet of paper at your disposal. I will not be on campus at all during the last week and I will be at home in Chagrin Falls taking time out to do some housework and doing things with my full time job there."

Preston was good for taking a full load of classes and working a part-time job. Today was Tuesday and it was his day to be on call at OSU hospital as the Chaplain. Preston really felt that he didn't want any calls, because it was usually over someone that wanted a newspaper at two in the morning, even though it was the nurse's job to handle that. It was a good job, just for the simple fact that Preston got paid just to hold onto a pager no matter if he got called or not! No matter what the money was rolling on in for a graduate student. Preston just sat back and thought how the Lord blessed him and his wife from virtually having nothing to sleep on, to being able to go to school, have two vehicles, and two jobs. He could remember those long nights as an undergraduate at Ohio State when he use to have to work at UPS from 10pm-3am Tuesday through Saturday and then go straight to a Saturday morning computer class from 8am-12pm. Thank God Preston enlisted in the Army so that he could get away from working from working for $8.50 an hour throwing boxes in and out of a truck with supervisors just yelling to go faster and faster like they were the ones doing all of the work. "Life sure does have its twists and turns" he began to ponder into one of his infamous daydreams of philosophical thought. "*Why does God make it so hard just to get where we need to go. If I knew I were going to do so many things before hand, I would have never been in undergrad school for five years nor would I have taken out so many loans to accumulate all of this debt for wanting to be an educated brother.*" Some of the brothers back at home call it wanting to be "white" for hitting the books. I call it staying out of slavery. It's so sad to look out the window at so many brothers and sisters that have warped their entire lives around twenty six inch rims and Cadillac Escalades. "Those vehicles are gas guzzlers, and who wants a guzzler during a recession? I will never come to understand the day where it actually makes sense for a brother to continuously sag in his pants like some toddler that has "doo-doo" all in their diaper. It just doesn't make any logical sense for someone to walk abnormally and wear your shorts like long pants in the summertime." Preston just shook his head in confusion as he looked up and down Main Street on his way back to Longs' house. "If this is the future that I have to look forward to, I am not so sure that I really want to see it" Preston thought in oscillating fashion. *It's a good thing that you are married and living in the same house as your children; it's just something we fail to see in America anymore. In some respects, that is the very reason why people envy you and your wife. You two are doing something that Christ loves and what the world hates.*

That was an encouraging thought, despite the fact that Delight has been running him up the wall since last night. Sometimes he felt like he was working more than one job, because every time he worked hard at making her happy she always found something negative to say about *something*. Pulling up to Longs' house in his Chevy Cavalier Preston already knew he had to turn around because one of Longs' playmates already took up the driveway stepping up to his door in stiletto boots and freshly manicured nails and open toe shoes to show off her pedicure. Lisa was up and at him as soon as she drug herself up the steps in a seductive state. *Frankly I don't know why he just doesn't marry the girl. She cooks and cleans his house everyday and she is over his house everyday before and after work. I never knew someone so dedicated to just making someone happy. His mom and dad loves her, but I think he is just trying to find the perfect that is out there, even though that person does not exist. If there were such a thing as perfect, I am sure there would be no reason for God to exist. After all, wouldn't that just defeat God's purpose?*

Preston and Lisa both knew this drill all too well, Preston would go and act like he forgot something, say hello to Lisa out of respect and march back on home; because Longs was the only person Preston ever thought was worth hanging around. "Hello, Miss Lisa", Preston waved from the open window in his car.

"Hey nerd number two, next to my number one", Lisa hissed sarcastically rubbing on Longs chest. Longs whispered in her ear so that he could come to the car and make parting words with Preston.

"Hey black man, you know what it is, Lisa got some tricks planned for me to help her out with so give me a holla once you get settled in at home." Preston and Longs both knew they both weren't going to say anything to each other once Preston's car started to head back up Winchester Pike.

"Alright man, take it easy and I got some viruses I need you to check out on my laptop, I'll call you." Preston had a sign of defeat on his face. . . . Now he had no choice but to go back home and listen to his wife, to pick up right where they left off this morning.

Chapter IV

"*Alright, if that's the way* he wants to play, then we are definitely going to have a long talk or his behind can sleep on the couch for the rest of the week. He is going to stop disrespecting me and treating me like I am one of his little brothers or sisters and understand that I am his *wife!*" After Preston not answering any of Delight's calls all day she was frantic and really didn't know what to do with herself. All day she was cleaning and grocery shopping so that everyone could eat once the kids got out of school. There really wasn't much else going on during the day, besides taking care of the house once everyone was gone and to make sure none of the teachers called for any of the boys. "I don't know what I would do with more than two kids," she thought. "All of this cleaning after them, my husband, and the dog is a fulltime job. I don't see how any mom has the time to work when there is so much that needs to be done on the home front. But, I do know one thing . . . once Preston Brown gets through that door; he is going to have more than a little bit of explaining to do. I am tired of this bull crap every week. He is just going to have to understand that God does not like the way he is treating me and that is not the intention in

God's plan. As a matter of fact, I am so frizzled I think I am going to have to call his mom".

"Stop, because I already know what you're trying to do", Preston yelled bursting through the door before Delight could press talk on the cell phone. Shocked at his entrance she dropped the cell phone, and suddenly regurgitated her anger towards him.

"Let me tell you something Mr. Brown, I don't know who you think you are or what kind of game you are trying to run on me, but it is going to stop and stop right now! I did not walk down the aisle with you and move a quarter of the way across the country with you so that you could treat me like crap for the rest of my life. So whatever attitude you just walked in with, you better just turn it right on around and go out that door, change it, and come correct!" Delight snapped.

Now this was something that Preston could not take. As a man he could not just let a woman in his own house just wiggle her finger in his face and talk to him like she was running the joint. "What if my dad and brothers were looking at me right now", Preston thought. "They would just be like who trained this fool and where is his manhood?"

For Preston, at this point there had to be some leverage shifting and it all had to lean towards him. There was no way that this could go down like this all day long and there be no say so from the king! Preston just could not fathom the thought of being "down-graded" in front of the boys and his dog. He just put his hands down in his face, took a deep breath and sighed, "I am going to take a walk around the complex and when I get back I hope that at least dinner is cooked and that I can actually walk into a peaceful house to enjoy for at least fifteen minutes." Preston walked out and closed the door gently trying to keep himself composed so that they would not have another one of their frequent outbursts in front of the kids and have the dog choosing sides of who to bark at first.

Taking a walk was always a relaxing feeling for Preston, he could take in all of the sights and breathe easily. Most of the people that were outside always had a kind word to say or at least waved from time to time. The lakes were very beautiful during the summertime and the only thing that spoiled the mood was the maneuvering around the goose dung that existed all around the area. "Man, I don't even see how women live with themselves! If it's not one thing, it's always another. This world is crazy. I am sure that all of those preachers that I thought had it perfect at the crib are definitely getting chewed out just like I am. There is no such thing as a woman who can keep her mouth closed. I wish that I could just snap my fingers and have Halle Berry appear for a few hours and snap back whenever she began to get on my nerves." Preston felt that he cooled down enough and was ready to go back inside and face the music that awaited him inside his own castle.

As soon as Preston opened the door with the kids having their backpacks on the floor inside the kitchen Delight snapped, "Well, I hope you got the stupidness all out of your system and that you are ready to eat and stop acting like an immature punk!" Preston could not believe that after having such a pleasant walk where strangers were smiling that he was about to succumb to this melee that he tried to distance himself from to begin with.

Delight would not be denied that she ruled the household and that Preston had no choice but to comply. She knew it would be a struggle for him, but she figured that after a couple of years of marriage that he would finally get the point. What frustrated Delight even more was that he would not engage in the conversation once she demanded a response. If there was anything that Preston could do to tick off Delight more than swinging on her it was the silent treatment. Knowing that she could talk more than a little bit, she just could not contain herself to be quiet and drop the subject once Preston shut down internally. The more she talked to bring Preston in, the more it drove him to shut Delight out.

Preston could not think of anything else to do except go upstairs forget about dinner and pray in the closet for a better day tomorrow. As Preston got down on his knees to pray he knew it was the only thing that could shut Delight up. Once the "G" word came up that was the only thing that could draw a stalemate for an argument in the Brown household. But before Preston uttered the first word, the phone rang. . . .

CHAPTER V

"H*ey, what up Rafiki!*" Preston answered the phone in relief. Rafiki was Preston's twin that has done everything with Preston ever since their birth. Rafiki was a little darker, taller, and teeth shown to be a little bit whiter. The man was just sharp and the two of them together in the same place was something to marvel. The two of them would have went to the same college together, but Rafiki fell in love with his baby momma and decided to stay home in Jersey. Needless to say, the relationship didn't work out and Rafiki was now paying back student loans and working trying to get himself back into college. "Man, I was just thinking about you, what's good?" Preston began to walk outside to get out of Delight's hearing range.

"You know me man, I just keep it gangsta, never sleepin' and tryin' to get this paper."

"I heard that, I still can't get Delight to even get a part time job to help me out and she only doing the school thing just one day a week. I mean this is ludicrous! How does this sound? Grown woman with two kids and all she do is go to school one day a week! Not to mention we on food stamps and Medicaid. I could see if we were both ballin', but we both in school. I could have done this all by myself. So I'm just like I'm ready to be out and find someone that's at least trying to help me and not sit on me. She brings up all of this God stuff, but don't know she sinning by sitting on her butt when God gave her the ability to get out there and work!" It felt good for Preston to vent a little bit instead of just arguing with himself day after day and Delight thinking he's crazy when she catches him off guard.

"Brother, that's why I am just fooling around with these freaks that are trying to help me out. If they don't want to help me pay child support, then I am out. Like your boy, Tyler Perry say, I can do bad all by myself. These bills are crazy and I am just looking for a rich chick with family so that I can inherit my cut. But anyway, I got some vacation time coming up and I want to come on through. I was thinking about next weekend if that's cool with the both of you?"

"Word! That's what's up, because right now I need somebody to kick it with and Delight isn't doing nothing but trippin' out tryin to argue with your boy every chance she get. So yo, do it like this, come in Southwest from Philly on a Thursday morning and roll out like a Monday afternoon. That should work real good around my class schedule. Because as soon as you get in here, I am out like a "choo-choo" train steam rolling out the door."

"Alright my brother, I will do that on line like right now and email you the confirmation."

"Alright man, just holla at me when you get ready to come through."

"Alright man, be easy."

"Peace."

As soon as Preston closed his cell phone, put it in his cargo pocket, he saw Delight dart out of the blinds of the window as he proceeded back to the front door. "So what did Rafiki want", she asked in a surprisingly subtle tone.

"Oh, he said he's going to be flying in next week so get the house cleaned up like you know how and stay out of sight". Preston knew it sounded somewhat harsh, but he needed some type of statement to push her buttons so he just let it come out as vague as he needed it to.

Delight's eyes began to narrow and Preston knew it was on now! "So you did not think to consult me or even say let me check with my wife?"

"Look, girl as far as me talking to you right now that will wait until I am re-energized tomorrow and besides he finally got some vacation time at his new job and you know we really only get together once or twice a year."

Preston that was not a smooth move at all now you know you just fueled the fire and all of the peace that you have just built up is about to be diminished.

Delight tapped her fingers on the kitchen table and let out a devilish laugh. "Oh, okay I see where this is going; you want to make a b%$# out of me, well now you have her! Kids go upstairs while I talk to Daddy and make sure that you turn the video game up real loud we are about to have some very intense fellowship."

Preston's heart began to thump a little bit, because he didn't know what kind of rabbit she was about to pull out of the bag, but whatever it was he needed to be ready!

Chapter VI

As Preston waited in great anticipation of what the next emotional flare-up would be he played cool like he was filing his nails and breathed easy like he was just in a normal occurrence. He was a firm believer in the "don't let them see you sweat" technique. Although he could play such a role with the best of them, Delight knew that it was his coping mechanism for pressure situations. In essence, she had him right where she wanted him; quietly sitting down and no place to flee.

"So did you really think that this stuff you pulled would actually go uncontested?," Delighted interrogated. As she spoke to him she gently walked in tight circles around him while Preston just posed even more cavalier. "So, you just wanted me to show my tail and now you got it. This is another issue I have with you; when it comes to your family everything is okay, but let Delight's family say their coming it turns into World War III. See, this is what I'm talking about with you. When you do the same thing its okay, but when it's you that's the problem you never want to admit that you are wrong. You're not right! You are not right!" Preston would just not act phased at this point. His main concern was when she was going to be done, because no matter what she was saying it was not stopping Rafiki from visiting Columbus. But, out of spite Preston replied, "That's because when my family comes over it is only for a few days, but when your people come it's always a month, three weeks, or something crazy like that. You already know my introvert rule; if they are here for more than four days it's time to hand them the broom!"

"Preston that is besides the point and you know it. You are not the only one that has a right to make the rules in this house. We both live here and my name is on the lease just like yours-"

"But mine is on their first!" Preston interrupted. "Besides, whose pay stubs do you think they took to use on the rental application? Not to mention that I am the one who has to go out every other week and get a cash advance while you scream up and down every time we get into a financial jam, like you gonna be able to do something about it." Preston could just feel the rage building up inside, and out of nowhere he picked up a plate full of chicken and flung it into the living room giving the dog a reason to choke on a chicken bone.

Delight began to cry and just walked out of the house to gather her emotions. Preston never knew why she always went outside if she was the one always starting the heated conversations. She paced back and forth fidgeting her fingers and looking up and down rapidly. Finally, she came back in and dropped the bomb on Preston. "I'm two months pregnant", she whispered.

"Say, what?" Preston said in bewilderment. "How are you going to be pregnant and you're on the pill? I already know what you are going to say, you forgot to take them one day. You know my pops told me about women like you. Always throwing up the baby game to get out of a situation. Anyway, I take care of mine. So are we going to be having twins tomorrow? Well, isn't this a happy family. Two college students, on food stamps, two kids, with one in the oven, and only one working a part-time job. The classic black family of the new millennium!" Preston spoke sarcastically.

"Well if it's what God wants, then we have no say in the matter. We'll be alright. I just want you to start respecting me like I am your wife, that's all", Delight spoke apologetically.

Preston clapped his hands in applause, "You know what, this conversation is over and Rafiki will be here and the brothers will do it up like no other! Good night." Preston stomped up the stairs and plopped himself on the bed to go to sleep without taking a shower.

Delight was so mad at him all she could do was sit downstairs and watch television until she fell asleep.

Chapter VII

Preston couldn't believe it's been a week and a half went by that fast and Rafiki just called him from the airport to say that he has landed. Preston couldn't head down I-270 fast enough to get him. All he could think about was how much fun they were going to have and catch up on old times and get the latest scoop on what's what back in Jersey.

Preston drove up the passenger pick up aisle and saw his brother with a big grin on his face. Preston stopped the car and popped open the truck so Rafiki could load his bag. "What's up man, how was the flight?"

"It was only fifty minutes and the turbulence was none. I told you, if I had the money I'd make the trip to Columbus every weekend" Rafiki retorted reclining his chair in the front seat to relax. "So where are we going to kick it? You know your boy gotta get it in before he go back. The last time I was out here was for your graduation from O-State and the honeys were looking right. That's what I need a college educated lady that I can have a "non-ghetto" conversation with. No arguing, but talk about something that just matters in the world."

Preston rubbed his chin, while concentrating on the highway. "Alright, this is what we'll do, first we'll hit a couple of the bars at Easton, sip some down and then we'll fly right and hit something on Morse Road or 161."

"Hey man, you know me I'm down for whatever and I know it'll be on this weekend. So you think you going to be able to get the hall pass from the wifey?" Rafiki knew that Preston might stutter on this point, but knew he would cook up something. Rafiki always admired the way that Preston could strategize and critically think as easy as water leaking from the faucet.

"You know what, this is what we'll do. We'll chill, do the family thing the first day that way she can get all of the trippin' out of her system and if she isn't done by then it's even more reason to get out and party." Rafiki liked that idea and just made him marvel at the ideas that Preston could come up with to make everyone settle down; even if it was fake. Preston was his number one pick for president (even if Senator Barak Obama was looking like he had a chance as the first black president).

"Alright, sounds like a plan my man. Now let's go see the fam and play with the nephews."

CHAPTER VIII

T*he weekend trip was* going pretty good and instead of staying indoors one day, Preston and his brother decided to stay in for a couple of days. The family games were great and the drama was down to a minimum. At least all of the outbursts between Preston and Delight were behind closed doors. That was the way Preston always preferred it. He couldn't stand the way that Delight's family always televised their business in front of everyone at family gatherings, baptisms, weddings, or anything else public for that matter. Preston just could not fathom the thought of getting into another intense argument in front of his family members with her. One, it would just make her look bad and two it would make everyone question Preston's judgment in his selectivity. Preston pondered all day when he should tell Delight what him and Rafiki have planned. *Preston just get it over with now. The longer you wait the worse it will be; so just tell her before she decides to make any other plans. You know how women are when it comes to having company and family.*

As Preston began scraping leftover mashed potatoes and corn into the dog's bowl he decided to let the bomb drop. "Uh, Delight . . . Rafiki and I are going to be stepping out tonight to get some drinks and do the brother thing. I know it's short notice, but I have to let him enjoy himself as far as the night scene and let him see some lights and action. He leaves early in the morning and it's his last night so that's what we're going to do." *Here we go . . .* Preston said to himself with his back turned towards Delight.

With a look of abhorred reality she blurted out, "And to think that your behind would have said something with some decency. So you're going to leave me here pregnant, with the kids while you and Rafiki go off and have the time of your lives?"

"Look, all we want to do is to do the guy thing and chill and do what he wants for his last night here! I would appreciate it just a little bit if you did not disrespect me in front of my brother. See that's the problem I always have with you and your mouth. You can't control it and you can't control your emotions. Yo, Rafiki!" Preston chanted looking for his keys to the car "Bump this dog, we out this piece. Delight stay bright!" Preston slammed the door behind himself while Rafiki sat in the driveway waiting for Preston to make his exit.

Preston ran out to the car with a devilish grin on his face as he made his way toward the car. "Told you I would get that hall pass boy! It wasn't pretty, but things had to happen in order for happenings to happen. Know what I'm saying." *This is going to be very bad when we get back home. I really do not know how much more this marriage could take of this, but it will soon be done if there is no respect shown by either of us here.*

Preston went into every bar Easton Town Center had to offer on a Saturday night. It was a nice spring night and the air was filled with adventurous adults looking for that special someone. Preston was relieved to see some other women himself, because the one he had at home did nothing, but cause him grief for the time being. Rafiki on the other hand was having the time of his life. He could not believe all of the beautiful women that he saw half-dressed and giving him all types of flirtatious acts that he indulged in whole-heartedly. Everything from playing hard to get to motor boating his mouth in between the breasts of some naïve college student.

It pleased Preston that his brother was having a good time. He knew that it was hard trying to live on his own in Jersey and paying child support at the same time, with minimal college credits. This was not something that they could do everyday and it kind of saddened Preston that he decided to go to school so far away from home and not to be able to enjoy these times more often with his brother. After all, he was only nineteen when he packed his bags on the Greyhound to head West. But, Preston could appreciate the fact that being out on his own was definitely a great way for him to learn about himself and what standing on his own two feet was all about.

"Ow," Preston squealed rubbing the right side of his shoulder blade in pain. Rafiki was so tipsy at this time that he totally disregarded how hard he punched Preston in joyous exhilaration.

"Man, it is definitely time for us to go hit a club. I might catch a case out here, because this one broad I tried to holla at was only sixteen, but the milk in those breasts was screaming like twenty fivvveee."

"Alright, I got the keys now just hold on to me while we go fetch the parking lot for the car and I'll let you dance some of that liquor off." Preston hasn't been to a club in so long, that he forgot what it felt like to actually wait in line to get into a night club. Preston paid for everything and there was nothing that Rafiki could do to make him think otherwise. As they approached a crowd of cars that they saw at a nightclub on 161, Rafiki make him park immediately as soon as he got a glimpse of a few small miniskirts and shirts barely covering the nipples of the females.

Preston was excited and nervous at the same time. *How can someone profess the gospel be here among all of the heathens? This just doesn't even make any sense. You are already frustrated, the women in here are looking fine, and there is just nothing good that can possibly come out of this. The devil sure is letting his light shine tonight.* Preston wanted to turn back, but Rafiki was so excited that he couldn't find it in himself to disappoint his brother, so in Preston's mind they were already on the battlefield and there was no turning back.

"Bro, you know exactly how to find the spots and find 'em right", Rafiki roared as he got out of the car doing karate kicks as an affect of the alcohol reigning through his system. "Let's get up in here and do some damage."

As they walked up to the bouncers to get patted down, Preston could now remember why he stopped going to clubs as an older undergraduate student. All of the pat downs, ID checks, black lights, cigarette and weed smoke in the clothes was just not his forte anymore. After paying a ridiculous admission fee to get in; they both looked around for a table, but they were all crowded by people dancing and grinding right next to them. *That would be a fight just brewing to happen and ruin everything you have worked so hard for.* So they maneuvered with their two step toward the main dance floor. After doing a full recon of the place they discovered that they were the only two males dancing. While the rest of the females grinded up on each other and looking seductively at Preston he continued to groove by himself.

"Hey, you go that way and I'll go this way. That way the ladies or the fellas won't think we are gay", Rafiki yelled into Preston's ear as he stared at one of the females in his sight dropping it like it was hot with a couple of her girlfriends. After Preston saw that up close and personal, he knew for sure it has been a while since he been anywhere and he knew the devil was all up in his face with no sign of resilience. Rafiki was nowhere to be found, but Preston figured he could catch up to him right before they got out of there.

After about two hours of dancing and running into people with an occasional drink here and there Preston felt like it was time to call it quits. He saw Rafiki waiting by the exit and Preston already knew he was going to be there, because they often thought the same thing at the same time. It wasn't quit tight near the exit and all of the females were once again all around Preston and Rafiki fanning themselves in the air-conditioned hallway. Preston looked at his cell phone and caught a glimpse of the "drop it like its hot" girl walk right past him. *Don't do it Preston!!!!!!* Preston being the "gentleman" that he was had to open his mouth. . . .

CHAPTER IX

Preston walked up to the light-skinned female who looked as if she were a mix of Mexican and West Indian. It definitely wasn't Puerto Rican, because he knew Puerto Ricans back in Jersey and the traits just did not add up. All of her features satisfied Preston's BET fantasy of a video girl that had thick thighs, at least a C cup bra, and a rear end that jiggled more than a little bit with every step she took in her white stiletto shoes and her perfectly manicured nails that did not seem to be too flashy, but just right.

Rafiki hinted he was going to the car and Preston held up his cell phone to signal that he was about to get a phone number to close out the late night. Rafiki gave him the gentleman's nod and proceeded to go and pass out in the car. As Rafiki walked out, Preston he ran up behind the young lady and gently touched her elbow with his hand and asked her, 'What's your name miss lady?"

The young woman eyed him in an approving manner and elegantly replied, "Lustray."

"So, Lustray do you have a man friend or anything like that?"

"No, it's just me and my two girls." *Let the*

drama commence!

"Oh, okay so are you from around here? I'm originally from Jersey but I went to school at Ohio State and I am currently here in graduate school."

"Well, if you must know Mr. . . ."

"Brown, Preston Brown, my bad" Preston winced in embarrassment with his heart pounding out of his chest dealing with very unfamiliar territory.

"That's better. I'm from Cleveland, but I have been at OSU for the last six years, but I will be graduating next year with my degree in mathematics."

Preston nodded his head in shock, "So is okay if I give you a call every once in a while?"

"Sure, let me see your cell phone so I can put my number in there for you."

Preston fumbled to get his phone out while she was anticipating seeing what type of phone he possessed. She punched in the numbers and made sure her phone rang so he did not think she was lying.

"Mr. Brown, it was nice meeting you, but my girlfriends are ready to go and we came in a group so we have to get going."

"That's okay my brother is in the car waiting for me and I should be checking on him to make sure that no one takes advantage of him while he is in his drunken state of mind."

They both laughed at Preston's bland comment and parted ways before the nightclub announced last call. Preston felt a new type of self worth, but was scared as hell of how he was going to play this thing out. "The girl had a banging body and could speak impeccable English", Preston thought to himself. "Dang, I only got three hours before I can get a nap in and have Rafiki back to the airport!"

Chapter X

The sun was coming up and Preston was speeding down I-270 to get Rafiki back to the airport on time. For some reason Preston just could not get the picture of Lustray out of his head. Delight did all she could to give him an earful from the time they both came in the door, but it was no use. She could smell the alcohol and smoke on both of them so she just figured they were both drunk. Preston engaged in her assumption and acted just like she accused; and it worked in Preston's favor, because he felt that it would keep him from hearing her mouth.

They arrived at Columbus International Airport with forty minutes to spare and even enough time for a brotherly hug. "Did you see that girl I was trying to kick it to last night" Preston asked.

"Oh yeah, I don't remember her face too well, but I do know that she had a big ole butt and the breasts were full of milk for a brother!"

Preston shook his head in confusion, like there was a fog that persistently clouded his head. "For some reason, I can't remember her face, but if Delight keeps giving me hell on earth; I'll give her a call and see where her head is at. Hey man, be safe on that plane and give me a call as soon as you board and when you land in Philly. I'll give Mom and Dad a call and let them know you're on your way."

"Alright man, thanks for a hell of a night last night, I haven't had that much fun in a long time. Love you man."

"Love you too", Preston said trying to hold back his tears. He could not stand to watch Rafiki walk off into the airport so he just sped off and didn't look back. "What an amazing weekend" Preston said to himself. "It was wild and fun, but now I got to go back home and face my arch nemesis . . . the wife."

Preston could not wait to get home so that he could finally shower and really take a nap the way that he wanted to, but knew that would not be possible if Delight were still awake stalking the kitchen door.

Thankfully, as he walked through the door he didn't see any sign of her downstairs and Preston felt it was good that she was asleep. That way he could fantasize about Lustray dropping it down in the club with no interruptions! *You know Preston, once you lust with your eyes you have already committed adultery.* "Aw, whatever all I'm going to do is call her in a couple of days and have a conversation then just throw the number away like I never even knew her."

On another note, Preston had some other things on his mind too. He had to hurry up and get packed to do some military training at Fort Irwin in California in the next couple of days. So he figured he would get some time in with the kids when he woke up from his nap and have Delight iron and sort out all of his clothes. The day was young and there was plenty of time left to get things done in a timely manner so from then on it would be slow motion. "I already completed my exams early so there won't be any conflict with the grades, the work-study people got the memo, and it's off to making some of that officer pay on the West Coast with a maid to make my bed everyday" Preston thought in excitement.

"Man maybe I should take the dog out and call her right now . . . no that would just break the forty eight hour rule. A man never calls the day after he gets the number; that would just be suicide in a desperate manner. Let me just chill, get some rest, and focus on getting out of here with everything I need." Preston tried to shake her out of his head, but every time he tried all he could think about was how angry and frustrated Delight made him. It was something about that Lustray that caught his attention, but he just could not figure out what it was. He's been involved with plenty of beautiful women at Ohio State and his wife wasn't a slouch either. He just could not put his finger on it. "Well let me see if Delight will be generous in giving some to the young Lieutenant before he gets ready to pull out." Preston took a shower, crept up the steps, and could not believe what he saw in the room. It was Delight, both boys, and the dog all in the bed sleeping away like they were in a coma!

"Wake up, all y'all!" Preston barked to everyone including the dog.

"What is your problem," Delight said angrily. "And don't think you are going to get any just because you kicked everyone out, you should have thought about that long before you and your brother decided to go and hop the town to come back here having the hamper smell like trash." Delight took the covers and just covered her and rolled over like he wasn't even there.

Preston dumbfounded couldn't find anything to say, but smiled and said, "Alright that's cool with me, because ain't nothing that you can do, that the hand can't and I'll be glad when I step out of here on Wednesday.' He gently closed the door, went down stairs, and made his own breakfast to watch Sports Center on ESPN until he fell asleep on the couch in his robe.

CHAPTER XI

Chapter XI

Preston could not believe that it was Wednesday already and he had to get on the road early because his plane left at four o'clock in the morning Eastern Standard Time. Everything was packed and ready. Even though Delight was still upset with him, she still managed to pack his bags and made sure that all of his dress shirts were ironed for the Protestant worship services that he would attend on Sundays.

"Well, I guess this is good-bye for a few weeks, huh?" Preston said with his face barely touching Delight's in anticipation for a kiss eventually. This was a ritual for Preston to kiss Delight at the door anytime he got ready to leave for any type of deployment ever since he was twenty-one. "Try not to kill the kids while I am gone and don't fall down the steps. Kids help mommy out and make sure you get all of your homework done before you try to go outside and play."

"Yes sir", the boys responded in unison. Tiger one asked with tearful eyes, "When will you be getting back?" He proceeded to give Preston a hug.

"In a little while, but you guys have to take care of mommy while I go out and make all of us some money alright, so that I can take you guys all over the country and travel, okay."

"Yay!!" They all gave Preston a group hug and even Preston got a little lump in his throat for the simple fact that he had to leave again, but it felt adventurous to him and it made him feel good that he could actually provide for his family every now and then without any public assistance.

The airport was never crowded and Preston felt like it's been a daily commute for him within the past week. There were people in uniforms from all over the world and he could tell which ones were off into a combat zone, because they did not seem happy at all. They are so young, Preston thought to himself. "I thought I was young when I was twenty-one, but these kids look like they are barely seventeen. These kids can barely shave and there is no body fat to show there is any type of maturity. Just as wide –eyed as the night owl, what a shame to not know anything about politics, but readily accept the role as a toy soldier and not know anything. I'm sure God has a plan for them, even if it is in Iraq or Afghanistan."

Time was going by slowly and Preston got tired of flipping through the internet on his cell phone so he contemplated calling Lustray. *Here's where it all starts. First the thought, then eventually the action. Just like a writer and a screenplay, this is where the movie starts.*

"Oh what the heck", Preston squandered. "The worse that can happen is that she will hang up on me, so I might as well get it over with. I'm not even sure if I was drunk or not fooling around with Rafiki, she might be looking like one of those VH1 freaks or something. Let me see what's up."

The phone rang and Preston began to fill with excitement. All he could think about was her droppin' it like it was hot in the club. As he continued to listen to the ringing of the phone he forgot one thing . . . her name! "What the heck was her name? I know it began with an "L", but was it Lucy, Lavena, Luscious, dang it I hate when I do this." Preston hung up the phone quickly in deep embarrassment once he heard a soft voice on the other line.

"You know what", Preston opinionated to himself "I am out here all alone, I might as well have myself a little bit of fun while I am at it. I'll just call and ask for "L". He flipped open the phone like he was Don Juan and hit redial.

"Hello", a soft and pleasant voice avowed on the other line.

"Uh, yeah is "L" there, I'm not sure if I have the right number, but we spoke briefly in the club a few days ago."

"Oh, yeah is this Preston . . . Preston Brown?"

"Wow, you have a good memory I thought you might have forgotten all about me already," Preston griped playing the humble man role.

"No, I am sorry to disappoint you, but I am not the typical girl that you would find in the club. I was actually just out celebrating with some friends to celebrate my girl's graduation from Ohio Dominican University. That is probably the last time for a long time that I will ever be in a club like that."

Preston began to get a little flustered, because it was the same school that Delight went to. He wanted to ask names and what type of program, but he kept his composure and decided to keep the conversation to a minimum.

"Well, I am actually about to catch a flight out of town for some military work that I do while in school, but I just wanted to call you to let you know that I didn't forget about you and that I hope we can pick up this conversation sometime soon within the next week or so."

"Wow, that would be great, just give me a ring whenever you get done doing whatever you're doing and good luck."

"Alright, cool I will do just that," Preston ignited in jubilee. "I have a feeling that we have lots to talk about."

"I am sure we do, Mr. Brown and by the way, the name is Lustray", she replied in a rather seductive tone.

Preston felt the way that she sounded; she could have the ability to ruin his whole life. Well, maybe not his whole life; but definitely the potential to do some significant damage. If he was going to perpetrate like he actually had a legal player card, his game would have to be tight. So the only logical thing to do would be to add himself to her list of many men that probably jacked up her self-esteem already. Preston never knew why that was always the case, but throughout his counseling in ministry many women would always blame their self-esteem issues on a man that didn't want to be with them any longer. If anything, Preston felt it was the responsibility of any one self to keep their self-esteem abreast. It was just puzzling to him that people always had to have themselves validated by someone other than God and themselves. But, he bagged the number, had the initial conversation and now it was time to board this plane. California love here comes Mr. Preston Brown!

CHAPTER XII

Back in Ohio, Delight knew that Preston was supposed to call once he was ready to board his flight and when she checked online to see if his flight were delayed or not; it read that it was on time. She just could not believe how childish he was acting over an argument that happened days ago. She called his phone and it went straight to voicemail, so it must have meant that he was in route to his destination. She just had to figure out what she was going to do with the boys for the next couple of weeks while she was pregnant and steadily growing tired and gaining weight.

Delight did as much as she could to keep herself busy the rest of the morning until she heard from Preston on her phone. So she decided to do his laundry and get that funky smell out of his clothes from the club that night. It felt good to finally have a washer and dryer in their new townhome. They have been through so much since they came from Jersey with almost nothing. She was reminiscing about the days they use to pack up the only car that they had with laundry, get the boys in there and haul off to the Laundromat. "God sure has brought us a long way", she exhaled.

She could never forget sleeping on an air mattress for all of those months, until they got their student loan money to purchase a queen bed from Original Mattress Factory. As she began to make the boys their favorite morning breakfast of pancakes and maple sausage she saw her cell phone light up with Preston's face on it.

"Hello, Mr. Can't call nobody when they are flying across the country."

"Yeah, hello to you too. Just calling to let you know that I am at my brief layover in Denver and everything is still on time. So I will call you once I have my bags in Cali, alright."

"Mmm. Hmmm. And please tell those skanks out there that they can only look at my husband and not touch him."

"I'll try, but they don't always listen," Preston said giggling. "But I gotta go so I'll call you later okay."

"Alright and I'm not playing about those skanks in the airport and around those military bases either. I love you."

"Peace."

Delight could never understand why Preston could never say I love you first. It was always her that had to say it and to get him to say it, she had to pry it out of him, which made it unauthentic once he did muster up the gumption to say it. Now that her nerves were calmed down just a little bit it was easier for her to sit down and relax without anything weighing on her mind. Although the money was good, she could not stand it when he was gone on those long tours throughout the years at thirty to ninety days a pop. It was bad enough that he was already gone for school trips to get credit for school and now the military had to come and interfere with her marriage. "Well, they do say that once you marry a soldier you are having a threesome with the government."

It pained her to see the kids crying over their dad being gone for long periods of time, but she always made sure that she reassured them that Preston was doing it to take care of the family and that he was out helping change the world.

She figured, part of the payoff was that since he became an officer they were able to afford a better apartment and didn't have to worry about saving quarters every two weeks for laundry. For some reason she had an uneasy feeling about this tour of duty he was on, but she could not figure out what it was. Maybe, she was just concerned about how things went down the last week Preston was at home before he left. In consolation she decided to call her friend Vashti, who she went to school with for the past few years at Ohio Dominican. She dialed Vashti's number and studied the scenery outside the patio window.

"Delight, what's up girl, what you doing calling me on a Wednesday morning?"

"Preston left and you know how that is, good money and no lovin'."

"Shoot, last time he came back you had a new wedding ring and a new car, if I had a man like that he could stay away as long as he wants as long the check was going into our account. All I get is child support and live with my mom and wait for my Tony's dad to come pick him up every other weekend."

"Girl, you are crazy so how is Tony's dad doing, despite the fact that you two work at the same building practically."

"Brandon is doing pretty good and I must say he takes care of *all* of his kids no matter what the situation is."

"Well, that's the main thing, because I can tell you with these two here I can't believe the affect that Preston has on them every time he steps out the door. Preston makes sure that the boys have everything that they need and he even treats my son better than our biological son sometimes. I guess that's the way he was raised, because his dad had thirteen kids and I had no problem meeting all of them. His dad made sure that they all knew each other and he has videotapes for days of all of them.

Girl, he must have been slick, because I don't know any man that has thirteen kids, four mommas and does not pay one dime in child support."

"Girl, all I can say is he must have had nothing but the good stuff to keep all of them quiet, because I know if I didn't have a ring on my finger, I sure enough was going to get a cut of a check!"

"Alright, girl well I'm going to get back to a nap so I can get my pregnant behind up to get some work done." Delight began to yawn into the phone as she stretched out on the living room couch.

"Y'all pregnant, I knew you were coming to school a little too happy. That was the problem, you were getting too much sex! At least somebody around here is. Before you know it you and Preston might end up with thirteen."

"Don't put that curse on me I am okay with just three after this one I am A okay. Anyway, the boys will be bored while Preston is gone and if Tony is looking for a place to hang out, he can come over her for a bit if he wishes too. I would invite your daughter, but there's just too much testosterone around here to enjoy anything besides watching television and playing videogames."

"Oh okay. Well he is looking for some playmates during the daytime so we will hookup later in the week."

Delight felt good that she had at least one person to call a friend while she was still recently new to the Midwest. Almost everything she did just comprised of her Preston, and the kids. It was kind of like they were the Goodfellas. All parties, trips, and special events just consisted of the four of them. No outsiders, no outsider friends. The birthday parties were just not the same as they were on the East Coast. There were so many more family members that lived within blocks of each other and everyone from her former job at the state school would all pitch in and drop their kids off to add to the fun. Those days were over and she just felt it was God's way of already prepping her for the military life that Preston was indebted to serving for at least the next six years. But, she figured that if they could make it through their three year long distance relationship while Preston was in his early years of college, there was nothing that they couldn't make it through.

Chapter XIII

Preston finally landed in California and just needed to catch a cab to get to Ft. Irwin. He was supposed to be taking part in some Chaplain training with a few infantry and Calvary units, so he could get some good marks to qualify for a Clinical Pastoral Education slot next year.

"Man, if I get a CPE spot next year the Army has no choice, but to put me on Active Duty and that would mean big money and a retirement all for serving the Lord. What better job in the world could there be?" He didn't want to ride in a cab, but his orders prohibited him from renting a car, so for the next couple of weeks he would have to rely on public transportation. Preston felt he needed to lose a couple of pounds anyway since it's been a couple of months since he has had some consistent PT. Studying full-time at odd hours of the night and working two jobs just did not always fit workouts into the equation. This was a time for opportunity and development. Besides, he always wanted to go back home and impress his wife with a better physique than he had originally left home with.

There were a line of cabs waiting for passengers along the curbside and all of the military personnel in uniform were being greeted by family and friends. Preston jumped in the first cab that he spotted and instructed the black African driver with a cigar in his mouth to drive to Ft. Irwin Main Post Chapel. The driver had a thick Nigerian accent and could not get over the fact that Preston use to be Muslim then turned into a Christian minister.

"Well, you see I was part of the Moorish Science Temple of America, which had more of an ethnic purpose and was founded by Prophet Noble Drew Ali in 1913 A.D. There was no such thing as black and white, in the Moslem faith we referred to them as Asiatics and Europeans, you know what I'm saying. So we really knew about everything that was in the both the Bible and Quran since all religions have a little bit of each of them intertwined in each other."

The cab driver scratched his head with his ebony colored finger nails, "So what you are saying is, is that this Prophet Noble Drew Ali is almost the same as Jesus in your current religion?'

"Not exactly, because Jesus in Christianity is not a prophet, but both fully God and fully man. Jesus was sent here in a man form so that God could show that he could humble himself even unto the point of death and reveal to the world that only God could overcome a physical death; as he shown after three days; subsequent to His burial. That's why we celebrate Easter every year." Preston loved to get into theological discussions about the Trinity, because that was the only thing that kept him from the Christian faith growing up. No one could ever explain to him what the triune God was until he had a conversation with Delight's pastor back in Vineland right before they got married. Ever since he studied it more fluently in seminary he just about became fascinated with the fact that he was a newbie in the faith and was really the only one that could articulate it with a logical tongue and ear.

"Brother, I think all of you Christians got it messed up with your three Gods and this human that you worship as God. Who ever heard of such a thing? Worshipping a man that people claim to have seen rise after three days . . . for all you know it could've been an inside job!"

They were getting ready to approach Ft. Irwin so Preston knew he had to wrap up the conversation on a high note. "That may be true, but as far as all of the studies and centuries of archaeological studies that have been done, there has never been a corpse found. And if one were going to believe in something, wouldn't be magnificent to know that you serve a God who could actually conquer death itself?" Preston's eyes widened as they approached the gate and he pulled out his military identification card for the MP. The cab driver passed through to the Army Lodging building and pulled over to the curb to let Preston out.

"Hey, brother I enjoyed our conversation and unfortunately, we have to cut our conversation a little short, but if there's ever a time you want to talk to a Jesus Freak like me, you know where to find me. I got it from here. And oh yeah, since I feel like blessing someone in the name of Jesus today here's a little something for you." Preston gave the cab driver a fifty dollar bill and told him to keep the change and have a blessed day! The cab driver looked at him in great gratitude and said, "You just might make me a believer yet."

He finally checked into his room and got situated and turned on the air conditioner the first chance he got. The rooms there were a lot bigger than any other post he has ever been on. The suites were basically one bedroom apartments, but cleaner and well maintained. That's what Preston loved about being an officer; he would be put in the best hotels the army had to offer. He could remember his days as an enlisted private when he would stay in billets for training and scrubbing floors with a toothbrush, just so that the NCOIC would find some soldiers to trample it just so Preston could do it again. How he wished that he could track down some of those NCO's now and just ask them if they remembered his name and rank from way back. But no, there would be no progress in it and after all his focus needed to be on the Lord and serving soldiers and their families. "Oh snap," Preston said to himself as he began to lie down on the perfectly made bed. He looked at his phone and saw that he had three new voice mails from Delight all within the hour he was supposed to get off of the plane until now. He knew that he was going to hear some type of hate mail so he just deleted the messages before he even heard them all of the way through and called Delight as soon as he cleared his voice box. Preston took deep breaths as the phone rang.

"Hey, Delight I saw that you called and my phone was still on silent, because I did not turn it off on the plane and then me and this cab driver got into it about my faith journey and the whole thing blew up and I had to do the check in thing and the unload thing, you know how it is" Preston huffed, trying to getting every meaningful word out before she could break in and tell him off.

"So, you're okay."

"Yeah."

"Bye." Without saying a word Delight hung up the phone on him and left Preston dumbfounded.

To Preston, it was a paradox of relief and shame. On the other hand he could not forget the pleasant conversation that he had with Lustray and the attitude he was getting from Delight was not helping him at all. So he made himself a hotdog in the microwave Delight packed for him, turned on the cable television set, hooked up the Ethernet cord to his notebook, and began to nibble on his hotdog in his bed and politic with himself about calling Lustray.

Chapter XIV

Preston's first day away from home continued to long on as she continued to clean throughout the afternoon and doze on and off. She was pretty much under control until she continued to think about the extra responsibilities she would have to endure. All of the football practices in the evening, calling all of the companies for bills to get paid, and the list just went on and on. She thought to herself, it's only a few weeks and every will be back to normal; this isn't the first time he's had to leave and he is helping to take care of the family. "*Well let me call Momma Brown and see if she's heard from Preston since he left this morning.*" She paused from dusting and dialed the 8-5-6 area code.

"Hello, mom? Yeah, it's Delight, listen. . . . Have you heard anything from Preston since he left this morning? He's wasn't acting like himself this morning and it seemed like something was on his mind since Rafiki came into town. I didn't want to bother him anymore and I was wondering if everything was alright with the family at home?" She knew she threw a lot in there, but for some reason she could not control her anxieties, even if she did try to calm herself down.

"Oh, yeah he texted me about an hour ago, but I haven't heard from him so I'll try to give him a call later. But, everything here back at home is okay. How are the kids doing?"

"Well, obviously they are not thrilled their dad is gone, but this is nothing we never dealt with before and I don't know if he told you yet, but we are expecting another little Brown within the next seven months."

"Uh, huh. Well, y'all just keep on doing it and you gonna have baby number four, five, and six. And don't bring any of them to me I got my two teenagers right here. But, anyway just pray and make sure the kids are eating and I'll try to give him a call and make sure everything is alright. We're on our way to choir rehearsal and I have to go all the way to Bridgeton so let me pony up. Bye."

"OK. Thanks mom I'll talk to you guys later." Delight loved talking to mom even though they clashed heads in the beginning of her and Preston's relationship. Mama Brown had a really hard time learning about her grandson when he was five months old, especially when her and Delight worked on the same campus! But, once Mama Brown accepted the fact that Preston was getting married; with no intentions of him coming back to Jersey to raise his family she really has opened her heart to love

Delight.

But now, it was really easy for Delight to talk to Mama Brown about anything that went on. Since Delight's mother passed away when she was five and no father figure in her life, except a grandfather; she more than appreciated the fact that she married into a family that was tight knit and had so much care for each other. She always felt Mama Brown could calm her down when her son was acting a fool and never could seem to get his act together in a gentleman's type of way. After all, she dealt with his father!

Now that the day was almost over, it was time to go to cook dinner, let the dog out, take out the trash, dishes, and laundry. "Lord, does it have to be this way every time," Delight thought to herself. Preston leaving was always toughest the first few days and all she could do was get down on her knees and pray in the midst of the boys playing the Playstation upstairs.

Lord, I am so tired and please give me the energy and strength to keep going on while my dear husband is gone. I pray that you use him in the manner according to your will and to use the gifts that you have given him only to glorify your kingdom! I am carrying another child and I pray that you make this pregnancy as successful as the previous two and to keep a close eye on this one as it is the first within our marriage. I pray that the days go by fast and that they are productive so just keep a guiding hand over me and fill me up with your mission statement every waking day. In Jesus name I pray, Amen.

Delight always believed that prayer was always the best medicine and that the devil was always a liar. Whenever she felt like she was overwhelmed she would read her way out of it, pray her way out of it, and learn her way out of it. There was nothing that anyone could say or do to separate her from her faith in Christ Jesus. Her prayers may not have always manifested itself immediately, but from past experience she was sure that there was nothing impossible when God was at the front!

Chapter XV

It was four thirty in the morning and Preston had already called Delight and it was off to PT to start off another Army day. Since he was working independently on his tour he worked out by himself until he had to report to the Main Post Chapel at 0900 hours. Preston loved to work out on a consistent basis whenever he could, because it gave him some sort of sculpture to his life physically. Whenever he trained, it caused him to eat healthier, stay awake during the early morning hours of the civilian world and ultimately he felt like he was glorifying God by keeping a perfect body active. He was always a firm believer that working out was a form worship, because he did not feel like God called human beings just to sit around and be couch potatoes!

"This sure does feel good to get my sweat on and feel human all over again", Preston exhaled wiping the sweat from his head at the bench press station. He never felt the day ever went completely right without devoting some time to the Lord and getting his PT in at some point during the day. Then the vague picture of Lustray popped up in his head. . . . "*Why can't I get that girl's frame out of my head?*" He didn't know her, had a brief conversation, and nothing more. "I think when I get done working today I'm going to give her a call just to convince myself that she's nothing to keep daydreaming about."

Preston flipped the phone around nervously as he flicked through channels trying to figure out what was the best time to call. Maybe around seven he thought. He figured by then if she was cooking he would know that she actually cooked and if she worked she would be home by then. So either way, it was a win, win! The time difference was going to be a killer though and then again; what did he have to lose?

Nine o'clock Eastern Time finally rolled around, so he called with great anticipation so that all he could do was think about that sweet, soft, seductive voice that played around in his head like a hit song on the radio 24/7. The phone rang and that sweet voice danced through the receiver as he expected.

"Well, hello there Mr. Brown the man with the plan."

"Hey, Lustray, I told you that I would give you a call and all I had to do was try to find the right time to call so that I could try and hear your voice a little bit." He knew he shouldn't have said that. That statement was maybe a little too forward and that would be a sure way to get shut down in the first quarter. *The deepest parts of your heart will come out of your mouth when the test of time comes.*

Quite the contrary to what Preston expected, she giggled and retorted, “Well I love the sound of your voice too. It isn’t the typical black man voice that I always hear so weeded out and sounding like nothing is going on upstairs. I saw you in the club, you look like you keep yourself in pretty good shape. So what do you do in the military.”

Now if Preston said he was a Chaplain that would just totally discharge him from the fact that he was worth being a Chaplain at all. How would that sound? Sitting in the club getting tipsy. *It would sound straight stupid so you best cut the conversation short and find yourself in better graces.*

The conversation went on for hours. They found out they were both in the high school band, loved classical music, loved to read, and even sat in the same class together in college and didn’t even know it. Preston felt like this was all too good to be true. Now he had this girl thinking that he was military intelligence and living in a single family home by himself with no children! He heard her sound so elated so he had to let the story keep going and he hoped he could remember every lie that he told her, because he was actually on the phone until he almost saw the sun come up. Being on the phone late that night he forgot to call Delight and speak with her before she went to bed! Well, it was alright, because if she were that concerned she would have called a hundred times like she usually does. But, wow this girl had her stuff together except for a couple of issues.

For one, she was still legally married even though her husband has been estranged for a about five months and two, she had kids of her own. Preston felt, if he did anything it would be real easy to just move in and move out with no strings attached. Okay it's wrong, but hey Bill Clinton did it, Martin Luther King did it, and even Thomas Jefferson did it! None of them seemed to be taken away from their purpose in life. But who knows, nothing might come out of this after all. *Now you know that you are just lying to yourself and that being on the phone almost until dawn is just like some old high school stuff that is just waiting to blow up.* Preston felt that she might just be down with the creeping and not really into that tie down stuff since she was already married. But, she has had her run- ins with men that have done nothing but broke her heart so Preston had to keep a story that would not tarnish that. For some reason he began to feel a sense of obligation to her since he was the "perfect guy" that had so much going on for himself and was not just someone that played sports and videogames, but actually used his mind! Lustray's acknowledging of this had done nothing but boost Preston's ego and made him feel more than secure. It was so much better than hearing all of that complaining from Delight back at home and how every time he did something there was something wrong with it. What was he thinking marrying her? How could he get so involved with someone that would tell him about his child when he was five months and give him the last name of the oldest one's father! "I was just too young to be getting married? I passed up all of these intelligent women to be with someone who does not appreciate me as a man and always feels like that I actually owe her something, because she had my child. *This is how it all starts Preston, the devil begins to work in tiny small steps and you won't even recognize it.*

Before Preston finished his tour of duty he came out of there changed man; not only physically but mentally. He would leave work early, not PT every morning and not even get his time in with the Lord. Instead of spending time with the Lord, he would talk to Lustray in place of his devotion.

He was getting off the phone in hurried conversations with Delight, saying he was working or had to counsel a family immediately and even managed to have Lustray call him every morning to wake him up.

The minister knew this had to stop, but how? How do I break her heart gently? Am I letting the love of my life go? What's really going on?

CHAPTER XVI

Chapter XVI

P*reston woke up tired after* another long night of dialoguing with Lustray. He felt like he was on top of the world and it's been the best he has felt in all of his life. In fact, speaking of the devil, here was Lustray buzzing in as turned over to reach his phone.

"Good morning, sir." It turned her on that he was actually an officer in the military and that seductive tone just sent shockwaves through his system.

"Well, good morning to you too", Preston moaned as he played with his hands in his boxer shorts, as if she were right next to him.

"It's only two more days and I will have to pick you up from the airport to chill with me. You are going to have such a good time, but you will have to stay trapped inside my room, because I don't want my daughters to see me with another man that I' am not married too. So how long are you going to stay?"

Wow. Preston was caught off guard with this one, but he had to come up with an answer quick. He really intended on coming by just for a couple hours then roll out in a cab to get his car from the airport. Thinking incoherently he blurted out, "two days." *Ouch. Now that he said that he would now have to try to explain to Delight why he is going to be home two days later.* This player card thing isn't as easy as it use to be in high school, but Preston was more than intrigued by the challenge. All he wanted to do was see if he could pull it off and then drop her like a bad habit.

"Yay," Lustray rejoiced. "That will give me enough time to cook you up a good meal once you get here and a good time for you to sit down and relax. I already told my family about you and they are interested in meeting with you sometime soon. I mean, just when I started to give up on men, when my husband use to beat on me and all the other ones that use to cheat on me in some form or another; it is really good to see that God made a man like you."

Darn, Preston stammered. Just when he felt he was ready to instill the cold shoulder role; he always felt more obligation to the role he established by Lustray's affirming words. Now what was he going to do? He never really felt like he had the heart to just dump someone like a stone cold player, but there was no way he was going to succumb to meeting the parents of some chick he barely even knew (even if the intent was to have an improper relationship right away). Hesitantly Preston responded, "Well, I don't think that it would be right to meet your people if I didn't meet your daughters first, so let's just take it slow to solidify the relationship first."

"See, that's why I like you. You are so thoughtful and intelligent, because I would have never thought of that, but it makes a whole lot of sense."

Preston fell on the couch and wiped the sweat off his head. "Okay well in two days it will be a date and maybe we can catch a movie or something while we're at it!" *Now why did you just have to throw that wrinkle in there, now you are just trying to get caught and embarrass the Father even further.*

"Well, hold up let me get my babysitters Brandon and Michelle a head's up so that I can let them know I will be finally be going out somewhere. So what I will do is pay them to keep them the entire weekend and we won't have to be too quiet if you know what I mean."

"Ok, cool. Well I will give you a call once I am en route to you." Preston felt a little stressed and excited at the same time. However, he did think that he has heard of the name Brandon before, but that couldn't possibly be the one Delight's friend Vashti had a son with. Besides, Preston wasn't a native of Columbus and who would know him from a can of paint? Anyway, he just had to call Longs and let him know what will be happening as soon as he touched down back in the Buckeye state! But, first he had to call Delight and come up with a plan.

CHAPTER XVII

Delight could not wait for Preston to get home so that she could just give him a hug and have someone to keep her warm at night. She has steadily been gaining weight and could not take chasing after the kids all by herself. The calendar was looking really nice as she was counting down the days for Preston's return back to the home front. *Preston has been working so hard over there,* she recited to herself as she began to think of plans of what to do once he returned. "*Maybe we could go out to eat, watch a movie, and maybe even just sit down and talk. That's something we haven't been able to do in along time, just sit down and have a conversation together. We can talk about the new doctor appointments I have scheduled and he could come along with me and hear how our baby is growing.*"

As the phone rang, she began to perk with glee as she saw her husband's number pop up on the caller ID. "Hello, honey. Are you ready to come home already?"

"Hey babe, we had a little thing happen over here, so the base is going to be on lockdown for a couple of days and I won't be able to get into town until a couple of days after we originally had planned." Preston projected his voice to sound saddened so that he would not give away his conscience while on the phone. He felt terrible that he was going through such measures to meet this other woman, but he had already dug such a hole that he didn't know how to get out of it. If he told Lustray that he couldn't go ahead with the plans, he would have let her down and would kill all of her hopes about her perspective of men and a damaging to his "good" reputation.

"What is going on? Are you going to be okay? I got the kids all excited and everything, and I have something planned for you."

"Trust me, I am more than sure that you would have something planned for me so I am sure that there is no way that I would miss another one of your surprises if I didn't have to. It's just a precaution they are taking, you know with the whole terrorism thing no one is taking any chances out here," he lied.

"Okay well just be careful and stay out of trouble."

"Alright, I love you and I will talk to you all later."

At that point she knew something wasn't right when he said I love you first and then a quick hang up. It all seemed uncharacteristic of him, but she just felt like she was being paranoid. Of course, she has been wrong before so it was no big deal. All she had to do was hang on for a couple more days and just do what she needed to do in order to make it through the next couple of days. At this point, it was back to business as usual so everything had to be done just like normal and to maintain her composure. As she washed the dishes she dropped a glass and it shattered all over the white tile floor. She couldn't help but to cry as she labored over head first to try and clear up the inconvenient mess.

"He better hurry up and get home!!!!!!!"

CHAPTER XVIII

Chapter XVIII

F*or once in a long time* Longs has not had any drama going on in his life. It looked like Lisa was giving the love and attention that he has always yearned for in a relationship. His mother and father were the classical example of what marriage was to him. Travelling buddies, business partners, and drama free! They were both retired and just cruising through life together without a worry in the world and that is the just what Longs has always yearned for.

The past few relationships for Longs were beyond belief and almost a soap opera to some extents. Preston could not count how many times he had to leave his house with his wife and kids, because Longs was ready to throw whoever she was out. For some reason this Lisa, made the cut to continuously make him a priority in her life. As Lisa and Longs began to make their way back home from a good day of running errands all over the East Side of Columbus Preston's ring tone came through to his phone.

"Wassup, black man?"

"Hey bro, did you kick Lisa out yet? I know she going past her quota of two months in the crib. Oh, my bad is the line secure?" Having the line secure was their way of speaking to see if it were alright to have a real man to man talk and to chop up the latest beef that has been going on in their lives.

Giggling, Longs signaled to Lisa that he would be outside on the phone to get better reception, which was really not the case. "Yeah, black man the line is now secure, what's cracking?"

"Well this broad I met at the club I met a few weeks ago at the club is banging and she is picking me up from the airport tonight!" Preston sounded so excited that he thought he was beginning to sound like own of those groupies that got back stage passes to a 50 cent concert.

"Hold on, hold on black man. You sure you want to run that route? Because you know if Mrs. Brown finds out it will be over for you. I mean you coming over here, because she already thinks I have too many women that come through for my own good."

"Well, the way that I got around that big brother, is that I told her we were having some sort of training exercise that put the base on lock down for a couple of days".

Longs couldn't help but laugh, because it was something he probably would have thought of back in his younger days of playing the game. After regaining his composure he thought and said, "Now since you are playing such a dangerous game at this stage in your life, do you have a cut off plan?"

"What the heck is a cut off plan", Preston questioned.

"Look, young head, if you are not going to be in a long committed relationship your young behind needs to have a cut off plan to get rid of her. So please tell me you have one so that I don't have to school you on that one too."

Preston felt real young at this point, because until Longs said something about a cut off plan, he really never planned it out. "Here's the curveball that I threw at ole girl. She doesn't know where I live and all I have to tell her is that I am deploying someplace across the globe and it will be all good."

"But you are still not listening to what I am telling you black man. You need to have a serious plan to cut her off or you will get caught up and there will be no return if you jack up your marriage. You have kids, a pregnant wife and there aren't too many brothers in Columbus that can say they have a Master's degree in their twenties and a career lined up as soon as they graduate. Look if you gonna get, get it! Because I know you're not going to listen to me anyway. So do what you going to do and make sure you get rid of her forever," Longs yelled a little louder than he anticipated. He really loved Preston and was always able to brag about him every chance he got. In some ways Longs felt that if he could do it all over it again he may have made some cleaner turns around the curb, but he was more than satisfied to be able to tell someone else the way it should be.

"Well, uh I thought you might be hyped up to hear a little bit, but now you make me want to not do anything with her," Preston said kind of disappointed at his exploitations.

"Look, I'm not telling you not to be a man, just don't jack up your marriage over something that's not worth it. Trust me I been there before and drama is not something you want to full around with when it comes down to it; especially when kids and money are involved. I have one seed and that was more than enough to go in and out of court about, but you my friend have two with another one on the way so just keep it simple and walk the other way. Being a player is dirty business and you have to develop a rugged heart to do so, so if you don't want that responsibility I suggest you abort the mission. I been out of the military for a while, but I do know the lingo."

"Hey man, thanks for the advice, but like you said I am going to get it, because at home it is not happening and if I do anything with Delight, it's an argument right after we get done."

"Black man, I'm not in your house, but all I know is that she loves you, because I get tired of hearing your name when I talk to her, so be cool and get back at me."

Preston figured he was getting into something with Lisa, because he hung up the phone rather abruptly, so Preston didn't even bother to call back. The way Longs put it, he felt like he was at a crossroads now. How do you carry on when your own boy doesn't completely have your back? Sure Preston knew it was sticky business, but he's been married since he was twenty-three! There was so much more he could be engaging in. What was the point of staying in a marriage that he didn't want to be in? Well, maybe he did like his marriage, but if he would've met someone like Lustray, it would have been twice as better! Maybe he should have been more assertive in college or more outgoing to explore some more. This was something of unfamiliar territory, but there was no way that he was going to be denied this challenge. He really did feel something take over him and telling him that being single was the best way to go.

CHAPTER XIX

P*reston finally touched* down at Columbus International Airport. He made sure that he wore his Under Armour shirt to accentuate his muscles in his newly trained frame and wore his best smelling Versace cologne, and his Sean John shades. He looked around to see if he could rapidly identify the attire Lustray texted him while he was landing. *"Okay, blue miniskirt and a spaghetti strap top,"* he whispered to himself. He saw one lady with a spaghetti strap top and thank goodness it was not her, because he did not remember her being that beasty in the arms. "That girl could threw me somewhere for a few rounds", Preston ruminated to himself. As he approached the exit, he felt someone pinch the left cheek of his butt and heard that delightful voice again.

"Hey girl, what you doing harassing people in the airport," Preston responded flirtatiously as he peered over his left shoulder.

"Well if its mine for the weekend, it's not harassment, it's consensual". She looked as good as she did in the club, and had some hips that she maneuvered very well with what she was wearing. All of the brothers in the airport kept taking double takes at her back as her and

Preston marched through the corridor towards the parking lot. Preston knew this was risky business to walk with a complete stranger compatibly in public where everyone could see them in broad daylight. Not to mention that they both went to Christian churches and there were people that knew them and their families. Obviously, Lustray didn't care, because she was on her way to divorcing her husband until she got the money to do so. But, Preston had other things to worry about; like how was he going to get out of her house and get his car from the airport without Lustray getting suspicious? Preston almost got a headache just trying to think about it, but as usual he was confident in his abilities to wiggle out of any tight situation that may come his way. After all, he was a young man that graduated from a college that was ready to kick him out! To alleviate some of the self inflicted stress on himself he decided that he would just focus on the evening and worry about all the other stuff later. He tried reminding himself that Jesus said don't worry about tomorrow, because tomorrow has its own problems. *Preston you know in your right mind that quote does not apply here and this can't go on forever!*

Lustray parked her Acura right outside the airport and Preston was ready for a night of mischief. "So are you ready for tonight", she hunched as she cut her eye at him and licked her teeth.

Nervously Preston responded, "Well, I'm down for whatever, I don't have anything to do for the next couple of days." He wondered how far she was thinking about going. Then Preston began to have second thoughts. He began to think that maybe it could be some type of trap and he wouldn't be able to make it back home to his wife and kids. Then again, she could be a super freak and have mad girls over there just wanting to get down with the get down for a wild weekend. Preston seriously denied the latter and just focused on taking his time and feeling her out, before he jumped to any conclusions.

Finally, they made it to the car and the inside smelled like peaches and cream with some Al Green on 98.9 FM one of his favorite radio stations in Central Ohio!

"See girl, this is what I'm talking about some nice mellowed out music to just chill. You're my kind of people" Preston jingled as he bopped his head to the music playing moderately in the car.

The ride to her place was only about ten minutes and if he didn't know any better they looked like they were headed in the direction to where he lived! *Oh no this is too close, she gots to get cut off at immediately!* Preston looked down at his wedding finger to make sure that the tan line from his wedding band was not visible at all. He felt that he did a pretty good job not wearing it for the last couple of weeks and just bathing it in the sun so there wouldn't be any conversation about it. Preston almost felt like he just wanted to tell her everything, but the joy and excitement on her face gave him a warm feeling as he overheard her bragging to her family and friends about him.

As they sat in the parking lot of the apartment complex waiting for her to wrap up her phone conversation she glanced over at him, hung up the phone, and said "You know what . . . I am in awe of your presence. You look even sexier, than you did a few weeks ago and even a little smarter than you sound. I think it's very attractive when a man such as yourself could be so gifted physically and possess so much intellect."

"All I can say is that it is God given and I do what I can, there is no one but God that has control over any of this stuff I have been blessed with." Oops! Preston began to chastise himself for sounding too preachy, but he thought he could work on it.

"We're herrrrre," she sang as she got out of the car and walked up to the house to open the door with her key. "I had the girls play at the park all day today and tired them out so there will be no interruptions while you are sleeping. If you need to take a shower the towels are upstairs and dinner is already on the table with some wine. I already had a little bit so you better watch out! I am going to change so I will be out in a minute."

Preston was in awe himself the way things were laid out for him. "This girl is well organized and really *can* ruin my life," he gasped to himself as he saw all of the asparagus and lemon pepper chicken neatly placed on his reserved plate with a candle burning in the middle of the table. He was really tired after the long flight so he figured he would just go to sleep right after he ate and took a shower. That was until he saw what would freeze his eyes in their sockets a few minutes later. The next thing he knew he saw Lustray come down in a fishnet outfit with some black stiletto boots that just made his manhood rise up like the Chief of Iron Fist Indian Tribe! Suddenly, Preston could not concentrate on his food and could not believe that he was getting ready to be someone's sex slave for a whole weekend. Preston never received this kind of treatment at home and all he could think about was using the nicely cooked dinner as an aid for the late night festivities.

Preston stopped eating abruptly, looked at Lustray, looked at the plate of food and asked,

"Do you mind if we kill two birds with one stone and shall we say have dinner and make magic at the same time?"

Without any hesitation Lustray blurted out, "I'll take the cranberry sauce and wine", and ran upstairs as fast as she could with Preston following as he took all of his bags upstairs so her daughters would not ask any questions in the morning.

The mission for Preston this weekend would be "Incognegro"!

Chapter XX

Preston awoke the next morning to some oral activity on his lower anatomy and looked at his watch as if he really needed to know what time it was. He could not believe he was actually in the same town as his wife and kids and them not knowing that he was there. If Delight found out any of this she would straight hinder all of his natural abilities. But, Preston could not think about that right now, he had to work on the mission at hand so that he could neutralize the target and make it back to home base safely.

After he recuperated from his morning glory, he was greeted royally with a big plate of French toast, some scrambled eggs mixed with ham bits, and just the right amount of orange juice. "This girl can burn", Preston whispered to himself as he ate splendidly. All he could think about was that he needed to leave this girl alone or he would mess around getting fat trying to eat three meals a day from *two* women.

Later the same day, Lustray dropped off her kids to Brandon's house so that her and Preston could go out to eat and catch a movie. This finally gave Preston a chance to finally turn on his phone, check to see who called and maybe even sneak in some time to go ahead and have a quick conversation with Delight. He peeked out the window so that he could see Lustray and the kids get into the car so he knew that it was safe to take a quick shower and do what needed to be done to stay on task. Preston hated the pressure, but loved his newly found adrenaline rush. He grabbed some towels, jumped into the shower, finally used the bathroom and dug out his cell phone from under his bag like he was an 1849 gold digger!

He checked the phone and was thankful no one called him at all. He was grateful that his wife listened to him anytime that he spoke of anything militarily; Delight had a great respect for the profession he chose and even more aptitude for his ministerial calling.

He called Delight anyway and was happy her phone came up to voicemail after about three rings. "That's right, she said she had the day planned with Vashti today so that's cool, but I better leave a message anyway so that she doesn't call me back while I'm out." So instead he decided to text her: EVERYTHING IS FINE AND I WILL BE BACK HOME TOMORROW SO I WILL TEXT WHEN I GET READY TO GET ON THE PLANE AND CALL YOU WHEN I TOUCH DOWN. LUV U.

"Excellent," Preston thought. "The home front was taken care of and all I need to do is figure out where to go for dinner and a movie where no one would recognize us; even though I don't have that many friends in Columbus. I got it, we'll go out to Dave and Buster's way out on the Northwest Side and no one will ever recognize me there and I know a movie theatre right around the corner from there. That way we'll do everything in one spot and all we have to do is get on up out of there while it is still dark. There is no way I could have pulled something like this off in Brotmanville. Obviously there is only one street in the whole town so I am sure somebody would know my mom or dad back at home, hell it would probably be on the front page of the Daily Journal!"

Lustray pulled back into the apartment driveway and hit the alarm on her car to go inside and greet Preston. All he could do was think about how fly she looked getting out of the car with her Burberry sunglasses on. Preston was dressed to impress and smelled like a million bucks. He was even impressed by his new self as he reaped the benefits of a strict diet with minimal effort of physical activity. "It's time to get this show on the road," he preached to himself. Preston was off again!

Chapter XXI

D*elight and Vashti* had such a good time at Cosi with the kids. All they could do was laugh at the boys as their eyes lit up inside the huge movie theater. Tony was intrigued by the way that the 3D theater looked so real and the boys were awestruck by the whole thing.

"Hey girl, thanks for letting us use your military discount to get in here. Because I am more than sure that we would have not chosen to come in here with the type of funds we are working with and it looks like Tony had a lot of fun with the boys," Vashti said gratefully.

"Oh, you know it's no problem for me to attract a little bit of company when my hubby is gone. All I need to do now is go home and get me some more sleep and finally get a break from the boys when Preston gets back in town. I don't care if he was out there grunting it out with his soldiers he's going to get his butt back into Daddy mode and handle his business."

"Alright then girl, let me get out here and pay this parking fee so that I can get Tony over to his Dad's. Brandon loves it when all of his kids get together and he was nice enough to give me part of the day for the holiday weekend. You Brandon and his girlfriend are sup posed to have some his friend, Lustray's kids come over while she finally goes out after that horrible breakup between her and her husband. I don't think I ever told you about that, but remind me to fill you in about that later."

"Wow, I don't think you ever told me about that, but I feel her I know what it's like to have a man away for awhile and have to take care of the kids all by yourself. It's good that she is finally getting a chance to get out and enjoy a piece of life. So that's his friend and not his girlfriend's friend? I don't know that sounds kind of funny to me, but hey it's not my man and not everyone is me, so in the meantime Preston will not have any girlfriends coming into my house."

"Amen to that, I don't know what the deal is, but they been cool for awhile and nothing ever sprang up so I am sure that they have it all figured out. As long as they ain't trying to turn my son out, I'm okay with it", Vashti snapped. "Tell Preston, I said welcome home!"

"Okay," Delight winced. As Delight loaded the boys in the car and wobbled herself into the front seat, she took her phone out of her purse and saw that Preston had texted her while they were in the movie. "Thank goodness everything is alright over there and he can hurry up and get back," Delight exhaled. "Hey boys, Daddy will be back tomorrow and you all can drive him crazy why mommy takes a rest. Yay!"

She didn't want to bother him with whatever he had going on so just text him back: GOOD TO HEAR AND SEE YOU WHEN YOU GET HOME. LUV U 2.

Delight still had a little bit of a funny feeling about him getting home a couple days later and him texting I love you. "That's just something he doesn't do on the regular. But, maybe he's finally starting to learn and this deployment is going to be a new start for him."

Chapter XXII

P*reston was proud of himself* the way he made it through the evening half paranoid of everyone that walked through the door during dinner and at the movie theatre. He was relieved to be back at Lustray's and having everything already packed up and ready for him to go early the next morning. The cab was reserved and he didn't give Delight a definite time so he was in the clear to make up the perfect excuse that he wanted to surprise her.

"You know, I really don't want you to leave, but I know that you have to. But, I really just want you to know that I really appreciated the time that we spent together and that I look forward to doing this again sometime very soon," Lustray purred.

Preston's heart fell through his stomach and once again he was scouring for the right words to say while she continued to praise him. "My pleasure, I just like it when people enjoy themselves and that makes it all the more memorable. I mean, there's so much that goes on in the world that tells us this place is evil; so I figured why not grab the small victories while they're there," Preston shrugged confidently.

"You are such a philosopher! Where do you

come up with such intellect and linguistic art?" She continued to look at him as if he were some sort of statue in the Smithsonian Museum.

That reaction deeply concerned Preston, because he felt that she was getting too attached a little too early and that spoke, "too many emotional issues" to him. The good thing was that he was going to be on his way home and sooner or later she would get the point. Nevertheless, he was fascinated by her choice of words and her appreciative spirit. Not to mention, that the food he ate sat inside his stomach all day, which was a meal that he could never turn down.

As they approached the house, he checked his phone to see that he did receive a text from Delight and that was good enough for the time being. "Oh, so you actually do have a phone," Lustray blurted out sarcastically. "I never heard it ring or anything, I was nervous for a minute and thought that you might have been one of those single husbands that I use to read about."

Now Preston was scared and perturbed! He just could not fathom that he could actually keep going on the way he was, because this girl was too smart. He could tell that she valued honesty and he could not fall into the trap of what he preaches against almost everyday. All he could think about was what his mom would think if she were to look at him right now.

Again, the sex was immaculate and intense. As Preston put her to sleep after such a long dual of physical activity he tried to sneak out of the bed, but every time he moved she squeezed onto him a little tighter. Preston made a mental note not to ever sleep over there again, because it was just too much of an exercise just to get away. He whispered to her that he was going to the bathroom so she gently let him go and whispered back, "You are the best lover in the world and your stamina is intimidating."

Preston would have loved to have stuck around and enjoy his ego boosting, but time was of the essence and it would be better to sneak out instead of explaining things later in the day when she would be fully functioning. So, as he used the bathroom, he redialed the cab that he had programmed in his phone to come and pick him up at a specific location down the street from her house so the lights from the vehicle would not wake her.

Preston carried all of his clothes downstairs and made sure that he was not leaving anything essential. He got dressed and was ready to peer out of the door just in time for the cab driver to arrive. He was glad that he didn't have to go too far so that he could save some of the loose change that he had in his pocket. The getaway car arrived and he was alleviated from all of the pressures that he had premeditated if something did not go right. "Now that's how you do it," he remarked to himself with immense confidence. "I got paid, got some, and got out that joint unattached." Now that there was some light out he needed to double check to make sure that he had everything in case his wife wanted to do her routine inventory to make sure that her baby got out safe with everything.

While switching everything over from the cab to his car he could not believe what he just did. He left his boots right downstairs in the middle of the living room floor for Lustray and her daughters to see! He was in such a rush that he forgot stuffing his boots in the duffel bag. It was too late in the game to turn back so he just focused on counting it as a loss and thought about retrieving them later on. It was time to get home to his pregnant Delight and his wonderful boys.

CHAPTER XXIII

Lustray awoke with her body sore all over. She could not believe that she held out without sex for over a year! "I have been missing out and I found someone who could throw it on me sternly! Mandingo Warrior! Whew! That was better than a roller coaster ride at Cedar Point and it was all for free." She looked around the newly arranged bedroom; default by weekend intensities and saw that the clock read 12pm. "Oh my gosh I have to pick up my girls. I told Brandon that I would be there around nine so that they could go out this morning." She could not believe that Preston left without saying goodbye or getting an extra round in before he left. "I was going to give him a special show before he left, but I guess he was just scared that I would bring the girls around him. He is so smart, but maybe too smart." She continued to look around and see if there was any trace of Preston and yes he did! "He left his boots so he would have a reason to come back to momma," she pondered during his absence. She got out her phone to call him to let him know, but all she got was the voicemail three consecutive times. "I wish I knew where he lived so that I could take them to him, but on the other hand, he's got private things to do, so I'll keep the working man to his business while we try hooking up later on this month."

She threw on a pair of sweat pants on to pick up her children and made her way to Brandon's house in one of the most chipper moods she has been in years. "I must admit, it does feel good to have a man in the house; even though he snores I love that too.

Pulling up to the house, Lustray could see her girls peeking out of the curtains awaiting her promised return. She walked up to the house with a big grin on her face until she saw Vashti trying to carry on a conversation with Brandon. She knew that Brandon didn't want her, so she could not figure out why she was acting like he really wanted anything to do with her. In Lustray's mind, if two parents weren't together, there was no need for any in depth conversations. Lustray always felt that she has been through enough in her life and that gave her the mature edge over everyone her age. This did not necessarily qualify her to be all and tell all and she knew it. But, for whatever reason she just could not grasp the concept of broken up couples being friends. Forget about being friends, she was even a strong advocate that married couples should not share last names or bank accounts. This may have well been her own prejudice from her current marriage and how it devastated her totally until Mr. Brown came along.

"Hey, Vashti, how are you doing? I see Tony is getting some quality time in with his father."

"Too bad I can't say that about your kids," Vashti though. But politely responded, "I'm doing good, but hoping I could be doing as good as you did this weekend. Hair all wrapped in ponytail, hat on, and some sweat clothes, looks like somebody got some!" Vashti had a way about putting people's business out in the street in perfect dialogue so there could be no repercussions since her statements usually flowed like water and no doubt telling the truth.

Reluctant to share any names Lustray sneered and signaled to her girls to get in the car, "Alright Brandon, I'll call you and thanks for watching the kids over the weekend." She knew that would drive Vashti up the wall and chuckled as she threw the car in reverse on her way out.

"She's finally in a better mood nowadays since she met that new guy. All she does is smile like she's on top of the world. Whoever he is, seems a little low key, because I never met him and she said she never been to his house, so I guess she got it under control," Brandon exhaled.

"Now you know if she met somebody and

gave it up like that, don't know where he live, she ain't nothing but a backyard ho! Jezebel at her peak!"

"That's just a little uncalled for, so what do you think my mama and all of them call you? It sure ain't saint, because you and I were just a sentence in a paragraph together and that was it. So before you go on talking about someone, make sure you check where you been too. Everyone has their own story so until you know hers I don't want to hear anymore nonsense at my house about the people I am associated with. Now that that's out of the way, I will be enjoying my son with the rest of my children for the remainder of the time that I do have. Thank you," Brandon grabbed his son's hand and slammed the door in Vashti's face as she stood there perplexed by his striking comments.

With nothing left to say, she just pulled herself together, walked to her car and drove back home to her mother's house.

CHAPTER XXIV

Preston finally made it home as he pulled up the house he saw his entire family waiting on him. Before he pulled into the driveway he remembered to throw on his wedding ring so that there would be no questions asked. He figured that he would probably order it a size bigger so that he wouldn't have to give his hand an extra tan anymore. He tried to convince himself that he was going to implement Longs' plan of cutting her off; before things got sticky like gum in someone's hair. But deep down he knew that he would keep her number in his phone and that thrill he tasted was captivating even though he knew it wasn't good for him.

The boys helped carry his bags into the house and Delight made sure that everything was hung up neatly. Before Preston gave her a hug he made sure that there weren't stints of perfume of loose hair strands framing him. It was very comforting to have a stress free moment in his own house; although, now he had to devise a plan to keep Lustray from calling him. "How was the trip?" Delight asked with curiosity.

Preston thought that she might have known something was up, but he had to remain calm for fear of giving himself away. "It was just like any other trip, long and boring, with free drinks for those in uniform."

"Oh so if it was long and boring, why don't we get *long and exciting* in the bedroom and throw on a movie for the kids to keep quiet," Delight purred as she tugged at Preston's collar, luring him up the steps.

Preston was already worn out from not sleeping the last couple of days and wondered if we would even be able to perform? So he cupped her breasts and spoke softly to her stating, "Babe, I had a long trip. So why don't we eat some lunch, take, a little nap, and go all out tonight."

While Preston hauled the rest of his things upstairs, Delight inspected his body up and down as he got dressed. Without thinking Preston jumped right in the bed without taking his ritual shower and Delight knew it.

"You're not going to take your shower?"

Preston wanted to just kick himself. If it was this hard to keep up such measures, then he didn't want to stay in this game for very long. Without missing a beat Preston shot back, "Awe girl I'm glad you said something I am so tired I forgot all about getting in there." Preston grabbed a towel and headed toward the shower feeling fictitious that he had to take a phony shower in his own house. As he took another shower he took the opportunity to inspect himself for any loose hairs and to get the smell of masculine soap on himself.

The shower did nothing but get Preston wet again and he began to feel like a slave to the game. *"So this is what it feels like to be in bondage . . . no freedom to love."* The shower took all of but two minutes and he immediately reached for the dry towel to cover himself in bed.

"While you get settled, I will make sure that the kids are alright and I'll be back up so that you can rub my belly!"

"Sure thing." Within the blink of an eye, Preston was sound a sleep for the remainder of the day and night.

Delight came back upstairs and tried to wake Preston, but he did not budge at all. She figured for him to be snoring like that he must have been very exhausted. So she decided to let him sleep while she went downstairs to read her Bible.

CHAPTER XXV

Chapter XXV

Seven Months Later

Ever since Preston has been home from California he felt like he has been running to the point of no return. He still managed to hold down two part-time jobs, go to school, help bring another newborn into the world, and keep Lustray on the side. But Preston could feel that it was taking a significant toll on his body.

"This nonsense has got to stop sometime soon. I'm just going to tell Lustray that we are done. She wants me to give her more time, more money, and I am about to be dry out of life. Well, Proverbs does say: Wisdom will rescue you me from a forbidden woman, from a stranger with her flattering talk, who abandons the companion of her youth and forgets the covenant of her God; for her house sinks down to death and her ways to the land of the departed spirit. I know that's right, because this nonsense is leading right to the middle of nowhere. I am just tired of stressing and lying to my wife telling her I am work when I am spending the night with her and her kids instead of my own. The sex is not all that any more and to sex two women at full force will just ruin a man's manhood not to mention low sperm count." Preston was kind of concerned, because Lustray has been acting very emotional lately and almost similar to the way Delight acted upon discovering her last pregnancy. He felt the day had come that he needed to end this double life mess.

The whole situation reminded him of Romans 7 his favorite Scripture in the Bible: For I do not understand what I am doing, because I do not practice what I want to, but I do what I hate. It was an ailing inside of him that crushed his spirit entirely. His sermons were no longer authentic to the people that use to invite him to preach and his body physically had become very weary and tired. So he just knew that he had to stop playing games and had to have a serious talk with Lustray. While Delight played with the kids inside the house he came up with yet another idea to get away to speak to Lustray on his cell phone.

"Hey, babe I need to go to the store and get some Motrin."

"There's some Tylenol right in the medicine cabinet," Delight demanded.

"No, but those always give me a stomach ache, I need some Motrin bad."

"Whatever, if you need Motrin that bad then just go ahead and go and get me something sweet while you're at it."

As soon as Delight got to the third word of her sentence, Preston flew out of the door and zoomed down to the Wal Mart parking lot to call up Lustray. He could not wait to get his cell phone out and make the call of death. He knew it would hurt her, but he was sure it was going to hurt him too. So he elected to get it over with and start the healing process. He dialed the numbers and prayed the words would come out as well as he rehearsed for the last two weeks.

When Lustray answered the phone he could not believe she was actually crying. What in the world could she be crying for? He feared the worse, but didn't want to start letting negative thoughts enter his mind. Preston took a deep breath and said, "Look Lustray, you know you're a special person in my heart, but unfortunately we're going to have to split up and go our separate ways. I know it's the holidays and right now I just can't give you what you want right now. I'm extremely busy and what you require of me I just can't fulfill right now."

Preston expected to hear a lot negative feedback and some odd marks of profanity, but instead heard nothing but a long eerie silence. "Are you still there?" He was hoping that she didn't drop dead, but felt she was far saner than that.

"Let me tell you something Mr. Brown, I went to the doctor today and I found out that we are going to have a baby! Yes you heard me correctly I am pregnant with your child. Now if you want to go ahead and be the typical, black, runaway daddy go ahead", Lustray roared.

Now Preston was the one with the long eerie silence. He didn't know if to cry or runaway. His hand on the receiver began to shake and his mouth began to dry up. He started thinking about his family at the house and what would they think of him. He kept trying to convince himself that it was a dream, but he knew that this was the real thing. *I told that there was no good that could have come out of this, you went on for far too long and the Word of God had to manifest itself. Now what are you going to do, knowing that you helped create this? She's still married, so your child is going to have her husband's last name no matter what; and there is nothing that you can do about it. You created this situation; you have no one to blame but yourself.*

All along while Preston listened to his conscience preach to him all he could ask himself was, "*How did I get here? I had it so simple and easy. I had a loving wife, kids all in one house, a career lined up to travel the world, and now it's come to this. Just having too much fun and got caught up in a life changing dilemma*" Out of panic Preston peeled out of the parking lot and drove straight over to Lustray's house. He knew Delight would be blowing up his phone, but he didn't care he had to know that this was the real thing with his own eyes. Preston always heard of this type of thing happening in the ghetto, on movies, but never thought this would ever happen to him. How did it come to this? It was just a conversation that escalated into a full blown relationship. He had to face the fact that he was leading a double life and there was no way that he could sugar coat it or make it look pretty.

When he arrived at Lustray's house the scene just looked like a horror. It was cold, dark, and the wind blew inexorably. The shutters at the house were cracking and every light in the house was off. Preston knocked on the door several times, but no one would answer. As he turned his back to leave he saw her silhouette shadow as soon as heard the door crack open.

Her demeanor did not look chipper at all, in fact she looked in total contrast from the first time that he ever saw her. Now her spirit was laced with attitude and resentment. Now that he was going to be the father of her child, he had no choice but to listen to her rant and rave as she pleased. For some reason instead of diverting from her, Preston began to feel more of a connection to her.

"Are you going to be a good father to this child," she inquired with a stark voice.

"What do you mean of course I am , just let me in," Preston began to force his way into Lustray's apartment as she tried to create a wedge between her apartment and the door, "now let's act like some adults and talk about this!" Preston could feel that he was losing grasp of the situation. "If I didn't care I wouldn't have come over here in the cold when I should be doing some work."

"Oh, I know what you do for work, you go on around playing Daddy and family man to your wife Delight and your three boys while I sit over here and get sloppy seconds. I know about your work preacher man."

Preston felt as if his entire face fell off and shattered all over the concrete porch. "Look, I wanted to tell you for so long but. . . ."

"But what, you wanted to get my heart first and have your child? Is that part of your game Preston? How many other mamas do you have running around here? You know what just go ahead and leave us alone we don't need you. I fell in love with a fake. I really thought you were different, I would give my estranged husband more respect than I could give you right now."

"Look I don't have any other mamas out

here, except my wife. I wanted to stop it for a long time, but I just got caught up and didn't know how to stop it. I guess making you happy made me happy, that's all and I didn't want you to think any different of me," Preston began to weep.

"Don't try to act like you're sorry now, the reason you're sorry for is that you got caught. I mean really how long did you plan on having this go on? I actually knew about your family for awhile Preston, but I just wanted to see if you were man enough to own up to it. Obviously not, I had to pry it all out of you. I don't know why men find it so hard to just tell the truth. If any of you had any balls the world would be a lot more settled."

This was a side of Lustray Preston never saw before. She was now raising her voice, wiggling all in the neck, pointing her finger at him, and talking down to him like he was some type of kid. Preston realized that she was upset and she had good reason for it, but in the meantime he had to figure when and how to explain to his family.

"Okay, I admit that I was wrong and everything. You were supposed to be a jump off, but you ended up being a lot more than I expected so there was no way that I could actually cut you off from the rest of my life. The main thing is what do you plan on doing? Are you going to have the child or not?" Preston could not believe that he just asked her that question and all he could hope for was that she was bluffing to get him to leave his wife.

"You know Preston, you must think that I am real dumb," Lustray retorted changing the subject, "every time that you use to spend the night over here, after giving you some good head, I would get on your laptop and read Delight Brown with saved documents on there. I read how she loves all of her sons and brags about her husband, Preston Brown," she snarled. "She makes me sick already. Oh so let me finish. Then, I went onto whitepages.com and found the address of you two living together. Then, I went on Google Earth to find out exactly which apartment you lived in. That's right, you don't have a damn house, you have a townhome!"

Preston had to think of a way to get out of this quickly so that he would at least have a chance at seeing his child. "We're actually separated and I am at the house; I mean townhome, she left and I am just trying to work on my marriage. So could you please stop the hauling and come to your senses for a minute?" Preston's cell phone began to ring and he knew it was Delight, because he was supposed to get her something sweet from the store over an hour ago.

"Aren't you going to answer your phone? If it is Delight, I can answer it for you and tell her where you are. Just tell her you're on call at the hospital like you always do when you come over here. In fact I can call her, I got the number memorized I dialed it so many times. Remember, that number you use to always see and no one would say anything on the other line? That was me calling! My stage name was Susan when I decided to say something. I was the infamous telemarketer your wife kept hanging up on!"

Preston was at a loss for words and to prevent further argument he just remained silent and took in the rest of her venting frenzy. His phone continued to ring and Lustray continued to rave. He began to feel like he was being attacked by the both of them so he decided to leave where neither one of them would be . . . Longs' house.

Preston decided to head to his car with an empty heart and defeated demeanor. Lustray yelled, "Go back to your wife, your whore, your mama! That's all you do, you're like a prostitute that goes back and forth, back and forth."

Ignoring the additional attacks from Lustray, Preston got inside the car, and slowly drove to Longs' house. It's been so long since he's been over his house because he was so busy running back and forth between Delight and Lustray. On the way to Longs' house Preston contemplated on everything from suicide to divorce and none of the options looked good. As he rolled up the driveway he beeped the horn to see if there was anyone home and Longs came running out.

"What's going on black man, I thought you would be somewhere powering up your vitamins or something the way I last heard you were trying to juggle those two women," Longs joked. Longs could look at him and tell that something was wrong, because Preston didn't laugh or crack a smile. Fear set into Longs' eyes and he said, "What's wrong?"

Before Preston could not get the first word out of his mouth, tears began to stream down his face and he could no longer hold in the pain that he knew was sure to come. "Lustray is pregnant! The girl is pregnant with my child and I don't know what to do," he sobbed.

Longs never saw Preston cry before and he didn't know if he wanted to cry with him or smack him. With a soft voice and slight hesitation Longs asked, "Do you think Delight will take you back?" Preston nodded. "Well it will be alright then," he patted Preston on the back.

"Man, I thought about everything from suicide, divorce, to running away altogether. I don't know what I'm going to do. Now I have to think about child support, visitations, and all that extra crap that does nothing but keep brothers in the system."

"Now that you *do* have to think about, but all of that other stuff like suicide needs to go out the door and the rest of this stuff is just life. You may not like it and not have it all figured out but, it's just life. And you know I'm not feeling abortions either, because believe me I have been there and to this day my ex-girlfriend and I can not stand to even look at each other. I have been through three abortions coming up and when it finally came time for me to have a son he died after he was four days old, because his lungs weren't full developed. So, my brother after trying to play God, in essence I played myself, because I always took it upon myself to take God's children. Now I have to live with that the rest of my life."

"But all the stuff that we ever debated and talked about why our people are so messed up is the exact thing that I have just created."

"What you have to remember is that Jesus died for you too, and sometimes we need to have a little pain to be able to walk in the rain with our head up high. In the meantime, you are going to have to be a man, act responsibly, and do the best that you can. Look, she has nine months to go and anything can happen in nine months. So if I were I would leave Lustray alone, go home to the family, and do what you should have been doing months ago. If you would have listened to me earlier, you would've gotten some booty and memories and not have to go through this. But, hey everyone has to learn somehow."

Preston hated it when he was right and at this point he wasn't even sure if he wanted to be with Delight anymore. He could just imagine what it would be like if he tries to work it out with her. She would have to know everything and be everything and try to control the relationship between him and his child and that was just not something Preston was ready to accept. But he did know one thing. He had to go back home.

Chapter XXVI

Preston dreaded the ride back home; because he already knew he was gone far too long and he was not going to give Delight any type of explanation. He was too burned out emotionally to cook up another one of his now infamous excuses. What did he just do? How did he let it get to such a point? Preston now began to realize that even the saved are not exempt from the devil's trap.

The ride home was way too fast for Preston's like. "I guess time flies when you have to go somewhere you are not excited to encounter," Preston jumbled in his mind. Now, that this came to a head, he felt now would be the time to tell Delight that he had another seed on the way. But, no he couldn't! "This is just the beginning; maybe she will have a miscarriage or something. Nine months is a long time away. Maybe she is just lying to get me to spend more time over there, since her daughters look at me as a father figure and they like me. But, I did go up in there unprotected more than a few times. But, how could this even be possible? She said she was on the pill! Now all of a sudden around the holidays, she's pregnant. This is surreal, I need a drink."

Preston saw all of the lights on in the house and he knew that Delight was up with the baby and there was not going to be any escape of this confrontation. "*I might as well just be a man and go on ahead in here and face the music. I'm the man of this house. I run this!*" As much as Preston tried to build up some confidence inside himself he knew there was really no way to prepare for what might come out of Delight's mouth. All of the education in the world could not prepare him for this.

Simultaneously as he opened the door he heard Delight shout, "Where the heck have you been! I am up here with our baby that has a fever from teething and I have school work to do. You need to sit down and explain this one to me."

Preston inhaled and exhaled deeply with his hand on his forehead and sighed, "Look Delight I ran into one of the pastors from the church and we had a real deep conversation about my future. We were trying to get a timeline for my ordination and getting into some baptismal ministry." Preston was disgusted with himself at this point. Every time he uttered another excuse with the church his heart cringed. "*Why can't you just tell the truth? What is wrong with you?" You are so deep in Satan's trap and there doesn't seem like there's a way out. The world seems like it is caving in on you, but there is a way. Just listen to God and not yourself.*

Delight sat the baby down on the couch, put her hands on her hips and countered, "So you mean to tell me that it took you four hours to bring me back some candy and talk to a pastor from the church?" She twisted her lips to the side and looked out of the corner of her eye like she knew that there was something going on. She smirked and retorted, "You know there was some girl that called here for you, but then hung up the phone. There was no caller ID. She said she was selling something, but it sounded like a scam."

Preston's heart dropped through his butt, but tried to remain composed, "You, you, you know there's all types of knuckleheads out there trying to scam for something."

"Are you cheating on me? Because, if you are you better tell me right now."

"Now does that even sound smart? I am living on food stamps and working a job that pays me a quarter of what their salaried staff makes. I wish I did have the money to be able to cheat! You know what, I am just tired and I am going to bed, I'll see you in the morning." Speaking of money, Preston had to go hurry up and pay that cash advance he took out to get some things for Lustray's house. It was a good thing that he looked after the money or he would have been toast. But, he still used cash whenever he did anything with her so there would be no paper trail; just in case Delight wanted to do some online banking.

As Preston proceeded to walk upstairs all he could hear were the loud weeping sounds of his wife. He couldn't just go upstairs with her crying the way that she was so he turned around to go and console her. Any other time he would have let her cry, but the way that she let out was a cry of pain and severe anguish. No one hit her so Preston knew that it was genuine impairment. He stroked her hair and asked, "What's wrong?"

"You! You treat me like crap and all I do is worship the ground that you walk on. All I do is listen to you, but when it comes to something that I want there is no compromise whatsoever. I am thinking about moving to Florida with my grandparents with the kids, because I can't be here and there is no way that I can stay here with someone who refuses to love me." Her hands trembled as if she were being shot with a stun gun.

What happens in the dark will come to light. There is no escaping that. You might get away with it now, but like I said before there is no way that a man can go on living a lie forever.

"Look, I just have a lot on my mind right now. I'll make sure that I will make an effort to pay more attention to you and the kids."

Delight shook her head in assurance. This made Preston stay up longer than he intended. All he could figure to do throughout the night was to slowly peel away from Lustray until he knew for sure that Lustray was pregnant. He hated to do it, because he was so intentional on creating a new image of men for her, but it didn't seem like no matter what he chose it would create a detrimental conclusion emotionally, and possibly physically. Maybe she might consider an abortion and she just might not tell him.

Preston sat on the living room couch feeling as if he had been drinking all night, the way things have been swimming around in his head. He couldn't stop thinking about possible birthdates, how his pride would be crushed if he couldn't see his child, the gender of the child. . . . Or, would the child be born healthy? Would God have the baby born retarded for his sins? Will my child be unhappy for not having his father in his life like Proverbs 7 says? "This is just too much to start thinking about right now. Just go to sleep, wake up, and tell Lustray you are going to lie back for awhile."

Preston felt like that he was going to lose his mind. He could not fathom how he just administered character assassination upon himself. He was his own hit man and didn't even get paid for it! All the while he listened to his baby cry upstairs while Delight cried along with him to sleep.

Chapter XXVII

Preston awoke the next morning looking like a crazed beast. His eyes were bloodshot red from a lack of sleep and his head felt like it weighed a ton. His sole focus was getting to Lustray's house and telling her it was over until further notice. Forget taking a shower or brushing his teeth. He couldn't even remember the last time he ate; or even wanted to eat for that matter. Just thinking about the entire situation made him sick to his stomach. He snatched the keys off of the key rack and drove as fast as he could to her house. "All of this driving is killing me too. All of this back and forth with gas prices this high. This is ludicrous, I could be saving an extra forty dollars a month for all of this. This is why black people stay in poverty, making babies while on food stamps with somebody else that's on food stamps." Preston began to get mad at himself the more he thought about it as he drew closer to Lustray's house.

When he arrived at Lustray's place; just as he approached the door to knock, Lustray heaved the door open and began to jump and kiss on him!

"Girl what are you doing? Your daughter isn't even up for school yet," Preston said in protest trying to unclamp her legs from around him. "Look, I have to get my priorities straight and I am just here to let you know that we are going to have to call it quits for awhile. You know, until we know what's going on with the baby and everything."

Lustray continued to try and unzip his pants while on her knees, "So what's that got to do with us making magic like we always do? The damage has already been done so let's go Daddy."

Preston continued to back up and as bad as he wanted to get intimate he had to think about the future, just in case there was the possibility of her not being pregnant.

"Look, girl I just told you I'm not doing anything until I get myself together. You better start playing with yourself or something, because you and I are both married and there are some things that can and have went very wrong here. So in the meantime just let me know how the pregnancy is going and when the doctor appointments are," Preston yelled at the top of his lungs to let her know that he meant business.

"Did you tell your wife yet? You know the earlier the better," Lustray pleaded.

"No, I didn't so let me handle it."

"So when are you going to tell her? You created this, so you have to fix this. I didn't sign up for this. She deserves to know."

"Look, I came over here to say what I had to say and I am off to class. So just text me if something comes up." Preston held up his hand in resilience as he buckled his pants and made his way towards the door.

"But-"

Wham! He slammed the door behind himself and all Lustray could hear was his car pulling off like someone just robbed her bank of love.

CHAPTER XXVIII

"*Oh, hell no! There is* no way he is going to continue to treat me like crap, come over here whenever he pleases and impregnate me like I'm a piece of meat that he can toss off to the side!" Lustray's hormones were raging and it was bad enough Preston wouldn't give her any sexual satisfaction. Now she had just suffered the ultimate rejection at the expense of his wife. "I hope his wife doesn't think that this is going to be some type of happy ending while they just act like one big, happy family."

Lustray began getting all of Preston's clothes together in a box that she saved just for this moment. She snatched all of his underwear, his movies that he brought, and copied everything off of his flashdrive onto her computer before she packed that too. "I'll show him and his wife that they are messing with the wrong one. *Maybe if his precious, skinny, little wife finds out, she'll kick him out and he can come and be with our baby.* In fact let me write a little letter to the housewife and let her know just what he's been up to all of this time. Besides, she deserves to know. She pulled out a piece of notebook paper and began to write:

Dear Preston,

I am writing this letter, because you have not yet decided to make a choice if you wanted to be with our baby or not. I can not just sit around and let you have your way forever. I want to thank you for the all expenses paid trips to New York, New Jersey, the Bahamas, and Miami. I'll never forget all of the shopping sprees that you took me and my girls on at all of the malls around town. Unfortunately, this relationship has to come to a close, because you refuse to be a man. I am sure that you have a nice wife that you use to talk so badly about and I am sure that you two will be happy together once I am out of the picture. I will let you know when the baby is born so you will not have to worry about anything until then. I just know that somewhere deep down there is a nice man that I have always hoped for; that I have yet to see. You just can't go on living a double life forever and I will not continue to be the other woman. I hope that you do turn yourself around for the best and somehow commit yourself to being a faithful man. Now, that we are parting ways I will only be able to see you through the eyes of our son. Loving you as always,

Lustray XOXOXOXOX

PS. If you ever think about me, remember my picture will always be in the back of your wallet.

"Perfect. I will just throw all of this inside a box and make sure that I spray all of my perfume over his clothes and that will be that. Now let me get the girls up for school and get their breakfast ready. Mr. Brown will be in school until about two and that will give me more than enough time to get this over to his wife. Now what did I do with those directions I printed out?" She got everything together around the house and texted Preston about her immediate intentions for the remainder of the morning.

CHAPTER XXIX

Chapter XXIX

D*elight woke up a mess* after crying herself to sleep and just felt the sudden urge to just get up and clean. The day was partly cloudy, which made the cold air that much colder in Central Ohio. Now, that her and Preston finally talked she felt a little bit better about their marriage. The kids got themselves up and ate some cereal before they made their way to their bus stop next to the house.

"Me and my baby are going to have a good time today. We're going to take a bath, eat some cereal in the high chair, watch some Disney cartoons, and enjoy Daddy when he gets back," she giggled as she held their new baby boy in the air.

Delight had real high hopes for the day and she prayed that the weeks ahead would be better than the past few months. She walked around the house and looked at her and Preston's wedding pictures that hung in synchronized fashion. "That day was the happiest day of my life. Everything did not happen the way that I dreamed on that day, but it happened the way that it was supposed to." As she stared into the picture, memories of all of the hard work it took leading up to that special day. She went back down memory lane how Preston would coordinate plans on the phone and how her and the matron of honor would run all over Deptford, New Jersey trying to get photographers and disc jockeys. The years went by so fast and everyone was so much older now. As she wiped her hand over the frame of the picture she heard a mysterious knock at the door. She wasn't expecting any packages and Preston was in school. "Who could that be," Delight asked herself. She peered through the peep hole of the front door and saw a strange car.

After taking a couple of double takes and not feeling threatened, she slowly opened the door and heard a chipper voice say, "I have some things for Preston." The young lady carefully placed the box in Delight's hands with Preston's name written on it in big, black letters.

"Why the heck does this little hoochie have a box for my Preston", Delight thought to herself as she shook the box in curiosity. She wanted to have some more conversation, but the girl ran off so fast that she didn't have any time to say anything else.

Delight shook the box and it smelled like the same perfume Preston bought her for their wedding anniversary. She put the box onto the kitchen table so that Preston could open it himself when he got back. But, after a few minutes of those familiar fumes starting to fill her house and an odd young woman coming to their house and rushing off; something just didn't add up. "You know what, I am going to open up this box and if Mr. Brown has a problem with it all he has to know is that it was in Mrs. Brown's house too!"

She sifted through the box and was bewildered at what she saw. There were clothes of Preston's, underwear of Preston's, some clothes she has never seen before and even some of the socks that she's been looking for the last couple of laundry days. "Oh, no! Oh no! Oh, no!" Delight cried out hysterically. He hands trembled as she began to read the letter page by page in very detailed fashion. With every word her heart began to sink deeper and deeper inside of her stomach. There was no way that all of this could be true she thought to herself. "A baby? But, he promised me for life. He's supposed to be getting ordained soon? I am just going to call Preston right now. I know he better not know this chick or we have some hard times ahead." Nervously, she tried to dial Preston's number, but the sweat from her hands just kept taking her to the other keys that she was not intent on dialing.

The phone rang several times, but she got nothing, but the voice messaging system. She tried again, nothing but the voice mailbox. "I am going to dial him up one more time and if I don't get in touch with him, I know something is wrong." She dialed his number once more and listened to the greeting and she wailed into the phone, "How could you? How could you do this to us? I can't believe you! Why won't you answer your phone! What's wrong, cat got your tongue? You better answer soon!" After leaving three more voice messages of the same monologue she began to prepare the house for the ultimate conversation that would be had as soon as Preston made his way home.

Chapter XXX

Preston looked at his cell phone in class and could not believe what was transpiring before his eyes. First, Lustray delivering stuff to his house! Then Delight calling emphatically. "This has just got to be a dream," Preston mumbled to himself. Preston was so vexed by the entire sequence that he could not even hear what the instructor was saying. All he could think about was if he should go home or not. After the fifteenth call from Delight, then Mama Brown leaving a text it was time to go to Longs' house and to try and talk some type of strategy.

Within five minutes Preston rolled up the driveway, let himself into Longs' house and without speaking, just showed him the cellphone.

With wide eyes and an open mouth all Longs could say was, "Oh my God, oh my God, oh my God." He said it so frequent and so fast; he began to sound like he was talking in tongues!

Preston enraged, grabbed Longs by the throat and exclaimed, "This is not helping me, and this is a matter of life and death. What should I do here?"

"Black man, you know I have nothing but love for you but you know I told you to leave that broad alone while you were ahead. Honestly, I don't know what to say on that one. But, you better call your pops since he's the one with all those kids and don't pay a dime in child support. I know he got something figured out to pull that one off," Longs held his hands up defenseless.

"You know what; you got a point right there. Let me go ahead and do that." Preston dialed his dad and filled him in on the situation just to hang up the phone in disappointed fashion. He was hoping to hear that he should not go home, but it was more than evident that he had no choice but to do so.

"So what did pops say?"

"He said that I had to go home and try to talk it out. Honestly, I don't know if I go up in there if I will come back out alive. I mean forget Iraq and Afghanistan this is terror on the home front for real!"

"All I know is that I will pray for you my little brother and stay out of the kitchen. If there is anything that I can tell you that makes any more sense than what I told you, it is to stay out of the kitchen. That way you can avoid any pots, pans, or knives that may come about."

Preston paced back and forth heavily like he was strung out on crack, but knew deep down that he had to go home. He shook so much that he had rather have been dead to stop the internal misery. "So this is what it's like to be shook," Preston mumble to him self. All of a sudden he stopped, looked at Longs, took a deep breath, and smiled. "You know what; I'm the man and I'm gonna handle my business. I'm out and I will fill you in if I'm kicked out of the house or not. If I am I will be back here and if not, I will be on the couch. Peace."

"Little brother, you don't understand. You are not going to get out that easy."

"And why not," Preston asked looking puzzled.

"Because she wants to give you hell first, before anything happens. It maybe a night, week, or the rest of your life, but hell is imminent my brother."

With that note, Preston just shook his head and made his way back to the car. While driving home all he did was rehearse the conversation that he thought he might have. He didn't know if he should apologize, play hurt, or just get yelled at. "I have to know where her head is at before I head in there," he thought. So he dialed the home number and called her.

"Hello, and I know you are on your way home, because we are about to get real deep and you are about to explain everything to me."

"Well, all I want to know is if my stuff is out there on the porch yet?"

"Oh, no mister, you think that it is going to go down that easy, bring your self here right now."

This terrified Preston even more, because this was something that he totally did not expect to come to fruition. The ride home was once again too short and it was time to face the music. He pulled up to the driveway and began to walk very slowly to the front door, but could already see Delight pacing back and forth through the kitchen window waiting for him to come in. As soon as Preston walked through the door he received immediate instructions and he had no choice, but to comply.

"Sit down! Sit down right here as I read a little something to you from your little b---- today! She came over here making sure that I read a letter that was supposedly addressed to you, but I know the drill."

"No, I actually think that it was addressed to me-"

"You just shut up and sit down," Delight yelled. She read the letter to him and asked him about every detail that was written.

If there were ever a time that Preston wished he could inflict death by internal suicide it was now. He felt like he was being held hostage in his own home. All he could do for the remainder of the time was look at his little baby boy who tried to figure out what all of the hostility was about. Preston could still not believe that he potentially created a baby that was going to be only eleven months apart from his baby boy!

"So what were you thinking Preston? Was it good? Was it because she was thick? Come on, tell me, because I just need to know, what the hell were you thinking lying down with that," Delight demanded as she stood on top of the chair.

Preston figured that he'd better say something or it would never stop, or it could get progressively worse in a hurry. And if he did answer he had better be honest, because the cat was already out of the bag. "Well, yeah it was good, I mean, I guess there was a reason that I kept going back." Okay, just keep the answers short and sweet Preston kept reminding himself.

After Delight paced back and forth hysterically for a few minutes without saying a word; she grabbed her coat and said, "You know what, I just can't stay here any longer I am leaving you here with the kids and I will be at Vashti's. Good bye."

CHAPTER XXXI

Delight pulled up to Vashti's house at lightning speed and saw her there talking to Brandon as he dropped Tony off from his midweek visit.

At the top of her lungs Delight yelled out, "Girl, you will not believe what type of sugar just happened to me today!"

As Vashti listened to the story her and Brandon began to look at each other with eyes wide open. As Delight continued on she could tell there was some type of irony going on between the two of them. Vashti cleared her throat and stated, "Girl, I am sorry to tell you this, but that is Brandon's friend I was telling you about and I am sure that there is more that he could tell you instead of me."

"Well, Brandon get to explaining because I don't have time to waste," Delight hissed at him. By the look in Brandon's eyes he knew that he had better come out clean with himself dealing with three women, all at the same time.

"I don't know everything, but what I do know is that they use to go on some dates, trips, or something like that and Lustray would bring her kids to my house so that she could have a sitter for the time being," Brandon said choosing his words carefully.

"I need answers, so the best thing you can do right now is to call her and to tell her to come over here right now, because this is about to turn into one messed up family reunion," Delight amped in a New Jersey state of mind.

Subsequent to him dialing the number Delight snatched the phone out of his hand and began dialoguing with Lustray. "Oh he just sent you a text? Okay, well you know where I live so just meet me there in about forty five minutes and we will sit down with Mr. Brown and have a nice little chat. I don't have anything against you I just want to know the truth so that I can get on with my life." Delight hung up the phone, handed it to Brandon and sped off out of the driveway.

CHAPTER XXXII

P*reston sat at home not* wanting to move from the same spot he had been sitting in for the last hour. All he could do was flip through his phone wandering how he could convince Lustray that he genuinely cared about her. There was no way he thought that Delight would let him into the life of a child outside of his marriage. Being someone that was raised by his father, he just could not bring himself to the point of not being involved in the life of his own flesh and blood. After debating with himself for so long as he looked around the apartment he could only resolve to contemplate divorce. "That will be the only way that I could be involved with all of my children and not have any strings attached. They could all be treated fairly and valued the same. All of the preachers around here preach about being involved with their children and that is exactly what I am going to do."

After Preston came out of the bathroom feeling a little bit better about his decision, Preston could not believe his own eyes at the sight in his kitchen. It was Lustray, her girls, and Delight waiting for him at the kitchen table!

Preston opened his arms, looked to the ceiling and cried, "Lord, just take me now."

To be continued . . .

Breinigsville, PA USA
28 October 2010
248305BV00001B/1/P

9 780982 556405